WEASEL UNDER THE SUN

WEASEL UNDER THE SUN

KYELL GOLD

Weasel Under the Sun
Production copyright FurPlanet Productions © 2026
Text copyright © Kyell Gold 2026
Published by FurPlanet Productions
Dallas, Texas
www.furplanet.com

Cover art by Irene Huang
Interior design by FurPlanet Productions

ISBN 978-1-61450-697-3

First Edition Trade Paperback 2026

CONTENTS

FIRST STORY

Patio
To garden
Garden Storage
Sun Room 1
Sun Room 2
Patio Room
Odd Room
Drawing Room
Tradesman and Servant Entrance
Storage
Laundry
Sitting Room
(Closed)
Closet
Closet
Library
Gallery 1
Gallery 2
Closet
Sewing Room
Staff Dining
Servery
Dining Hall
Entry Hall
Foyer
Small Parlour
Large Parlour
Cook's Closets
Kitchen
Mister West's Study
Pantry
Cook
Asst. cook
Coal Room
Boiler

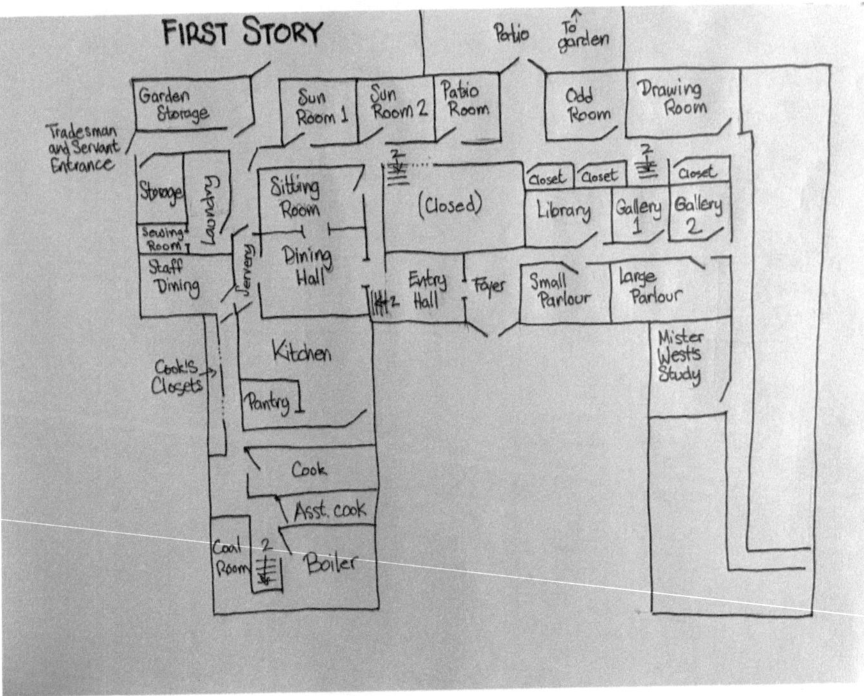

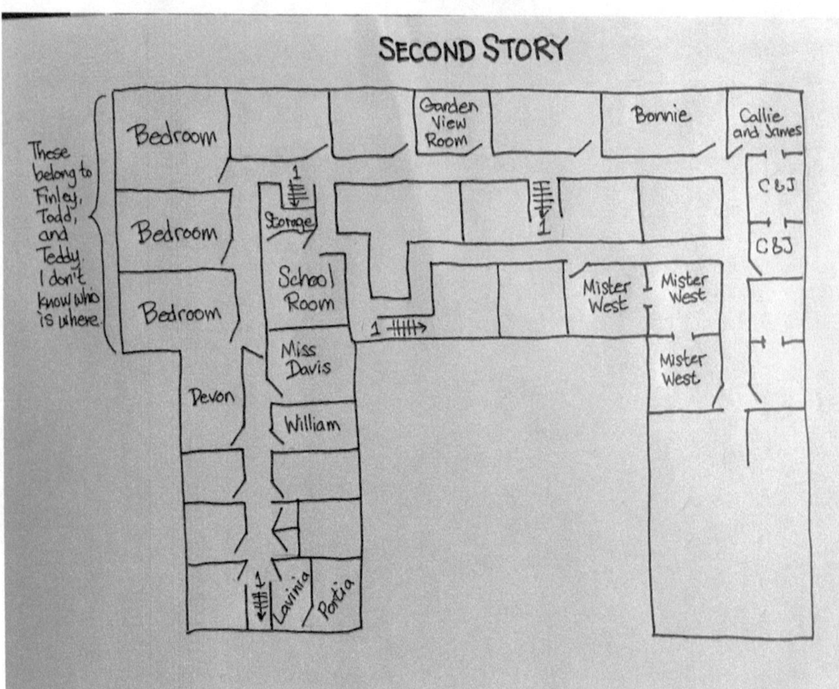
These belong to Finley, Todd, and Teddy. I don't know who is where.
Bedroom
Bedroom
Bedroom
Storage
School Room
Miss Davis
William
Devon
Lavinia
Portia
Garden View Room
Bonnie
Callie and James
C & J
C & J
Mister West
Mister West
Mister West

CHAPTER 1
WILLOW'S END

Miss Davis, the brown rabbit who ran the serving staff of Fortescue Hall—and thereby ran the Hall itself—met Ellie at the Willow's End railway station and appraised the shorter weasel with eyes as sharp as the grey dress she wore and the bonnet pinned neatly between her long ears. "So you're Miss Stone."

Ellie, very aware that her own small hat had slid over one ear and her blue dress was rumpled from the journey, clutched her luggage with both paws. "Yes'm," she said.

The appraisal lasted only a moment longer, and concluded with a small, "Hm!" after which Miss Davis reached out and took Ellie's case with one paw, hefting it easily. "Come along, then. It's over a mile to the Hall. I hope you're not afraid of a little exercise."

"No'm." Ellie fell into step slightly behind the athletic rabbit, almost jogging to keep up with her pace. They left the small station and walked quickly down the main street of Willow's End, which here seemed to be mostly business offices.

"Now tell me," Miss Davis said, hardly breathing hard at all, "how is it you come to our kitchen? Master Charles has told me you're an assistant cook for the Hathaways up in Widden's Crossing, and you're on loan to us while they're in Monaco."

"That's right," Ellie said, trying not to pant too hard.

"And why are the Hathaways not bringing you to Monaco?"

"Mr. Hathaway told me, ma'am, that the resort has its own cooks, and so all the cooks are being given leave."

"But you are being sent here." Miss Davis did not turn, but Ellie felt the sharp appraisal on her again.

"Yes'm," Ellie said. "Er, Mr. Hathaway would like me to get more experience in a well-run kitchen, and he said your head chef is very well regarded."

At that, Miss Davis stopped and did turn to Ellie, her ears cupped forward. "I see. So he intends you to take over the head cook position in a few years."

Ellie's small ears warmed. "He hasn't said, ma'am. But our head cook is getting on, and last month he made a chicken pie entirely without salt."

"Oh, dear. So this isn't a punishment for you."

"No'm. Although Mister Hathaway did say he hoped I would 'broaden my horizons' and learn some new dishes."

"Ha." The rabbit smiled. "You'll learn that from LeFou, all right. Just have a caution you don't learn too much more from him."

She set off again, and Ellie hurried to catch up. "I'm sorry, ma'am, what do you mean?"

"Oh, LeFou is brilliant at cooking. Not so much at other things, such as getting along with people, or courtesy."

"I see."

"Or minding his business. But you'll learn all that soon enough." Miss Davis pointed as they crossed to a smaller street, bustling with activity. "There's our greengrocer, and beside them the dry goods. If LeFou sends you out for ingredients, that will be where you go. As it happens, I need to speak to the greengrocer. The carrots he sent up yesterday were quite unacceptable. Yellow patches and far too thin."

Ellie fixed the two stores in her mind, but it was not hard to remember them. The greengrocer's canvas awning stretched over many small carts filled with carrots, lettuce, parsnips, vegetable marrows (these looked surprisingly fresh, considering it was summer; they must be from a hothouse). Next to that small brick building stood another, with "Dry Goods" prominent over the window in which Ellie could see fabrics and either salt or sugar, maybe both.

Miss Davis stopped in front of the greengrocer's with an imperious stare as though she owned the store and wanted to assess how assiduously the employees were working. "Well," she said, "it doesn't seem Georgette is busy. Come, I'll introduce you."

With no more explanation than that, the rabbit strode quickly toward the greengrocer. A badger leaning against the carrot cart stood straighter as they approached. "Good afternoon, Miss Davis, ma'am," she said.

"Working as hard as ever, I see." Miss Davis cast an eye around the carts. "I suppose Mr. Hochley doesn't mind if the carts aren't kept full?"

"You going to buy carrots?" Georgette asked pointedly. "If you're not, I don't see how it matters to you how full the cart is."

"It matters," Miss Davis said, her tone dropping some twenty degrees, "because I am in charge of Fortescue Hall, and we could easily bring our shopping in from Groveby if need be."

Georgette's muzzle dropped, and sullenly, she said, "I was just about to fetch more carrots."

"Of course you were. I shan't keep you. I need to speak to Mr Hochley, but before I do, may I present Miss Ellie Stone. Miss Stone will be assisting us in the kitchen up at Fortescue for a month, so if she comes by on an errand, please give her the same quality of vegetables you would provide to me."

"Of course, ma'am." Georgette met Ellie's eyes with something like sympathy.

"And there will not be so much call for you to come up to Fortescue yourself. At least for this month."

The badger's brow lowered for a moment, and then she put on an even sweeter voice. "Oh, Miss Davis, I don't mind goin' up to Fortescue."

"I am sure you don't. Still, we shall have more paws in the kitchen and perhaps with Ellie taking cooking duties, we can send William down to pick up the delivery."

"William." The badger's expression made it clear what she thought of William, if not precisely why.

"Yes, William. Now Miss Stone, wait here, and I'll return in a moment."

The tall rabbit had hardly passed the doorway into the store proper before Georgette said, "What is it this time?"

"Er," Ellie said. "Carrots, I think. Yellow patches?"

"Hmph." Georgette tossed her head. "Old bat can't unnerstand that veg isn't made in a factory, like. Whole house up there spoiled rotten, that's what I think. Want everything to be fine and perfect. Not everything's fine an' perfect. It's the imperfections make something interesting. Y'ever hear that?"

Ellie, taken aback by the flow of words, managed a short, "I do think I've heard that."

"You've got plenty yourself," Georgette said. She reached out to fix Ellie's hat, then looked down at her dress. "You must be quite interesting."

"I don't know about that." Ellie wasn't sure whether to be offended or pleased. "I'm just an assistant cook."

"Hm." Georgette looked at her shrewdly. "Someone who don't put so much stock in their clothes must be thinking about something else. What d'you think about?"

Ellie didn't want to mention the police novels or Abby, so she said, "Er, recipes, mostly."

Georgette's eyes narrowed slightly. "Maybe that's so. Maybe." She stepped closer and lowered her voice. "Listen. Anything you might want over the next month, but maybe you don't want the old prison warden," she nodded toward the store, "to find out, just get word to me. I take deliveries up an' I can add a few things here and there, no trouble." She winked.

"Like what?" Ellie asked, bewildered.

"Oh, never you mind." Georgette smiled. "Just if you happen to be thinking how much you'd like something but you don't want it delivered to the front door, remember you've got a friend at the greengrocer."

"I will," Ellie promised, though she couldn't imagine what she might want. Other servants had snuck things into the household: treats they weren't supposed to have, and certain magazines. But she'd never needed either of those things. And she wasn't sure how much of a friend Georgette was. Everyone in service had a kind of camaraderie binding them, but she wasn't even in service—not that she'd last long if she were, not with that attitude.

And then, as if sensing Ellie's uncertainty, Georgette glanced back into the store and took a carrot out of the cart next to her. She slipped it into the pocket of Ellie's dress. "There you are," she said. "Pity how that one wasn't fit to sell, but you can have it for later."

Ellie started to object, but just then Miss Davis came out of the store, calling over her shoulder, "Thank you, I shall expect so." She turned her attention to Ellie. "Well, come along, Miss Stone, we must get back to Fortescue."

"Pleasure to meet you, Miss Stone," Georgette said. "Nice that there'll be at least one person pleasant to talk to up there."

"Good day, Georgette."

"Good day, ma'am." But Ellie didn't turn quite as fast as

Miss Davis did, so she saw Georgette stick the tip of her tongue out at the rabbit. The badger met her eyes and gave her a wink and then disappeared back into the grocer's.

"You mustn't listen to her prattling," Miss Davis said. "She sees quite a bit of Devon up at the house, so at least she must find his company pleasant. Though I don't know what he could possibly see in her, if I'm being honest. Well, you spoke to her for a few minutes. You see what I mean."

"I suppose so," Ellie said. "Is Devon one of the family?" She only knew of the family that they were badgers like Georgette, and it would be something of a surprise if a greengrocer's assistant were seeing one of the family.

Miss Davis clearly felt the same. "Hah," she snorted, and then recovered her composure. "He is not. Nor is he under my supervision, more's the pity, or I would've put a stop to it." She hurried her pace as though wanting to leave Georgette behind. "Over here is the post," she went on with a gesture. "I don't expect we'll have occasion to send you down here, but if we do, there it is."

"I do write letters to friends of mine," Ellie said. It was the easiest way to keep in touch with Abby.

Miss Davis looked down her short nose at Ellie. "Do you indeed?"

The question did not require an answer; it was intended not to ask for confirmation, but to convey to Ellie what Miss Davis thought of young ladies who wrote letters. Still, the question had been asked. "I became quite close with a chambermaid at my posting a few years ago. We are both in different situations now, but I like to check in and make sure she's coping well. She's a tender soul and...and it is a violent world."

That last part came out rather without Ellie intending it to, but it was those words that seemed to strike Miss Davis. "It is indeed," she said. "As long as it's another young lady, I suppose there's no fault in it. Charitable, even, to look out for her."

"Yes'm," Ellie said. "Thank you."

"Speaking of your postings, perhaps you could tell me a little about them. This one where you met the chambermaid, this wasn't with Mr. Hathaway, I presume, since you are still with him."

"No'm. This was the posting before that. She and I worked for the St. Clairs up near Bushington."

"The St. Clairs...foxes, were they?"

"Yes'm."

"Then I suppose I needn't ask why your employment there came to an end. You were there for that dreadful business."

"I was, yes." Months had dulled the memory somewhat, but sometimes, for no reason, Ellie still saw Mr. Giles St. Clair, sprawled dead on the landing, blood dripping down onto the stair. The blood wasn't the worst part; the dead stare of his open eyes was the worst part. She had had nightmares—again, not so many lately—of discovering his body, the moment made somehow worse by knowing it was approaching.

His son John had tried to keep the household together, but in the end he'd sold the house, and he and his sister had split the money and parted ways, the staff given small sums as a thank-you and glowing letters of recommendation before being let loose to find their own way.

Miss Davis strode to the end of the street before speaking again, and then said, "That must have been terrible. But I assure you, you've no need to worry. Nothing of the sort takes place at Fortescue Hall."

This statement did not reassure Ellie very much, for it did not indicate to her that no murder would take place at Fortescue (an event she had not been very worried about) so much as it indicated that Miss Davis did not understand very well the reasons people committed murder, and therefore thought that she could, by imposition of her will, prevent murders from happening.

In fact, as Ellie now knew from personal experience as well as through her police novels, people committed murder for any number of reasons. It could be planned out in advance ("premeditated," they called it) or something that happened quickly and without warning; it could be over money or power or love. Still, it had been months since Mr. St. Clair's death, and although another murder had happened at Abby's house in the meantime, mercifully Ellie had been spared a repeat of that experience. "I'm sure it won't, ma'am," she said.

This street was lined with cottages on either side, and Miss Davis spent some few minutes on the resident of that cottage ("simply useless old shrew") or the one across ("let their cubs run wild") or the one at the end of the street ("spends more time at the pub than at home") before stopping at the end of the row of neat little cottages that Ellie had quite liked.

"On ahead here," she said, "there are more cottages, and then some farms. But here we go through this gate—which must always be kept closed, unless Master West is expecting company." With that, she lifted the metal gate from its seating and swung it open with her free paw. Ellie hurried through the opening, and Miss Davis followed and then closed the gate. "Now from here it's easy, even though you can't see Fortescue from here. This path leads directly to the front door, and you can't mistake it because of the wheel-ruts left by the carriages. Lavinia *will* keep going along one of the sheep-tracks and then claim she got lost, but that's poppycock."

The path did seem very clear, a brown dirt track with parallel wheel marks and well-tended grass on either side. "Who's Lavinia, ma'am?" Ellie asked.

"My daughter. She's a chambermaid here, and you'll be sharing a room with her."

"My friend is a little like that," Ellie said. "She does her work well, but when she's not working she has a tendency to drift off and dream."

Miss Davis sighed. "It is good you have experience with that sort of thing. If you can rein in Lavinia, I will be greatly in your debt."

"I'm sorry, ma'am, but what do you mean by 'rein in'?" Ellie asked.

The path led them up a small rise, where Miss Davis stopped just short of the top. She turned to Ellie. "I would like Lavinia to take over my duties one day," she said. "This is no secret. But she seems uninterested in the workings of the house. She performs her duties and then goes off to draw in her notebook—simply an excuse to spend hours doing nothing, so far as I can tell. Perhaps from a young lady of her own age—or about her own age—" Here was the first time Ellie had seen Miss Davis falter, only slightly, as she realized she had made an assumption about Ellie's age. She rallied quickly. "If you could impress upon her a need to understand the workings of the house, I would be most grateful to you."

"I see, ma'am," Ellie said.

"And I would like to remind you that it will be I, and not Master West, nor M. LeFou, who will write your recommendation letter at the end of your month."

"Yes, ma'am," Ellie said. She wanted very badly to receive a good report after her time here. "I see."

They proceeded on up the small rise, and there Ellie got her first glimpse of Fortescue Hall. The sight made her stop even as Miss Davis walked on down the path.

Before her spread out a large manicured garden. The path she stood on now, a dirt lane, continued with a sharp bend to the left, otherwise it would have run straight into the neatly kept lawn, criss-crossed with a grid of lighter-colored grass that Ellie recognized as "foot-grass," soft underfoot and durable, so it didn't get worn down as the more attractive lawn grass would by a continuing parade of feet walking over it. Flowerbeds lined the foot-grass paths, some of which were open to the air and some of which ran beneath rows of shade trees. Ellie spotted a statue of an angel, or at least some person with wings, that spouted water into a basin at the center of the gardens.

But beyond the gardens, that was what had stopped Ellie in her tracks. When Miss Davis had mentioned Fortescue Hall, Ellie had imagined a building like those she was used to working in, a three-story manor house with five to seven windows across and some fancy decoration around the roof. But Fortescue Hall looked like a palace to her. What she could see was laid out in a square, shallow U shape, with the base of the U facing the gardens. Elegant stone steps led from the gardens up to a stone porch with a railing, and large windowed doors let into the house from that porch. From where she stood, looking at the southeast corner of the house, she saw twelve windows across the base of the U, another nine on the wing facing her. And she knew there was another wing, because behind the main body of the house rose a square tower. A tower! And there was another tower to the left of the main house, this one with a cupola, as well as one overlooking the stone porch.

"Well? Well?" Miss Davis' sharp tone brought Ellie back to herself.

"I'm sorry." Ellie gathered her skirt and hurried down the lane. "I've just never seen a building so grand. It's very like a palace."

The rabbit smiled, mollified. "We are all very proud of Fortescue. Master West takes good care of it, and in fact the East Wing is being repaired at the moment. The Hall itself— come along, come along—is over 300 years old, and was last renovated a hundred years ago."

Ellie hurried to match Miss Davis's pace. They walked along the edge of the gardens, and Miss Davis raised a paw to a deer who was occupied trimming the bushes. "Hallo, Mr. Wilkins," she called out.

The deer looked up and raised his nose to the air. "Good afternoon, Miss Davis," he said, and went back to his trimming.

"You'll meet Mr. Wilkins at meals," Miss Davis said. "He's been here longer than I have, even."

Ellie stored that away as they kept walking, and then asked, "Is Master West a Lord?"

"He ought to be, by rights!" Miss Davis shook her head. "No; the last Lord Fortescue squandered his fortune and sold his estate to Master West's father in 1920. Master West controls most of that money still, and has made more of his own."

"Is there a family business?" Ellie asked.

"Master West has written several books."

She did not seem inclined to tell Ellie more about them, but Ellie's curiosity would not let her keep quiet. "I love books. Might I know what books he's written?"

Miss Davis stared ahead at the hall as she walked. Finally, she said, "You may have heard of *From Sumeria*?"

"I may have," Ellie said doubtfully.

"It's sold thousands of copies."

"Is it a, er..."

Miss Davis sighed in exasperation. "He travels around the world to dig up old ruins. *From Sumeria* was a book about one such voyage."

"And that's how he made his fortune?"

Miss Davis looked reprovingly at her. "We do not discuss our employer's finances."

"Oh." Ellie, who had done that with the staff at every other posting, laid her ears back.

The rabbit cleared her throat. "My dear, in a general sense you should know that you can't build a fortune on books. However, a successful author with a keen mind for business might turn a modest income from books into quite a sizable fortune, if he invests properly."

"And, I suppose, if he had money left to him by a wealthy father."

"Indeed."

They arrived at the southwest corner of the manor, and now Ellie could see the small door in the side that the lane ended near. But here Miss Davis stopped her. "Master West is kind," she said, "and an extremely intelligent fellow. He has built his staff accordingly. Many are not what you might call traditional help, but are quite competent. They might have difficulty finding a position elsewhere, but Master West allows them to flourish here."

"All right," Ellie said. "Like the cook? When you said he isn't good at getting along with people?"

"Quite so." Miss Davis looked pleased. "But the thing to remember is that we are all devoted here to Master West and his family, just as any other staff would be."

"Of course," Ellie said, wondering whyever she might be led to think that they were not devoted to their employers. Of course, not all staff were, but in her limited experience, the better the house, the more the staff bonded with the family.

"Good." Miss Davis looked satisfied to have settled that matter. "Now let's introduce you around."

CHAPTER 2
THE SERVERY

Ellie expected that she would be taken to the kitchen, but after entering through the side door of the grand mansion, Miss Davis did not take Ellie down the hallway that smelled of food, but past two sun rooms (she opened one to show Ellie, as it was too early for the family to be using them, and Ellie marveled at the gold trim and the large windows) and then down a cross corridor to what she told Ellie was the main entry hall, a grand space with marble floors and a wide dark wood staircase with gold trim. Portraits of badgers lined the walls, with the intermittent landscape depicting the surrounding hills and fields in between, and one unexpectedly of ruins in a desert. She realized as Miss Davis swept her past the paintings that that must be of one of the ruins Mister West had written about, in Sumeria, was it?

"Are we not going to the kitchen?" Ellie asked.

Miss Davis peered down at her. "How do you know where the kitchen is?" she asked sharply. "You've never been to Fortescue."

"I smelled it," Ellie said, "when we came in. And I don't hear a lot of people around, so I don't expect you have two kitchens, although this house is large enough."

"One of the kitchens is out of use." Miss Davis gestured ahead of her. "In the west wing, which is presently being renovated. We are going to see Mister West, as he wants to interview all new staff, even temporary ones."

So they passed down a narrow hallway—"This is the Front Hall. The library is there on the left, and farther down are two art gallery rooms. On our right is the small parlour and the large parlour." This brought them to a branch leading to the right, which Miss Davis took.

Down this hallway, most of the left wall was draped with cloth, and beyond a single door, the right wall was as well. "This is the west wing," Miss Davis said, unnecessarily, Ellie thought.

"The one being renovated."

"Indeed. And Mister West's study is here." The tall rabbit came to the door and knocked.

From inside, a deep voice said, "Enter." Miss Davis pushed the door open and stepped inside. Ellie followed and got her first look at Mister Charles West.

The study stretched easily twenty feet from left to right and probably fifteen from the door to the window. One wall was lined with bookshelves, another covered in framed maps from antiquity. On the large oak desk that dominated the room stood a globe that looked fifty years old, if not more, and a stone knife in a glass case. Behind the desk sat Mr. West, in his brown tweed suit with a yellow bow tie, wearing a pair of round wire-rim spectacles, and behind him stood a glass case with other artifacts in it, some pots and small statues.

The room smelled a little dusty; even frequent cleaning would not erase the smell of the old papers and books. But the open window behind Mister West brought his scent to Ellie: a very light fragrance of juniper and laundry starch. From that and the grey on his muzzle and ears, she suspected him to be in his sixties or perhaps early seventies; juniper as a fragrance remained popular mostly among the generation that had fought in the first Great War some forty years ago.

His smile when he met her eyes was broad and genial. "Miss Stone," he said. "Welcome to Fortescue Hall. It is a pleasure to have your company here. Mister Hathaway has spoken highly of you."

"Has he, sir?" Ellie was startled into saying. "I mean, thank you. That's very kind of you."

"Should he not have?" Mister West's eyes twinkled.

"He's free to say whatever he likes, sir," Ellie said.

"Indeed." He studied her for a moment longer, and Ellie had the impression of being one of the Sumerian ruins he'd uncovered. "Well, you will find us an easy house to get on with, though Miss Davis may not share my opinion of the kitchen." Beside Ellie, a small "hmph" affirmed this. "My sister and her husband live here with their three children and two grandchildren—both grown, there are no cubs running about Fortescue —and we are accustomed to breakfast at seven, luncheon at noon, tea at four-thirty, and supper at seven-thirty. Beyond that, your time is your own."

"Yes, sir."

"Have you been to Willow's End before?" Ellie shook her head. "What do you think of it, and of our little home here next to it?"

"It's lovely, sir," she said. "I grew up near Cambridge and have always worked near larger towns, but I quite appreciate the quiet."

"So did my father," he told her. "He bought this place after Callie and I had grown up, so it isn't quite 'home' to me in that sense, but it has become so."

"Oh, Fortescue Hall is so very grand," Ellie said. "I've never served anywhere like it."

"Thank you." He smiled. "Miss Davis takes very good care of it with the staff remaining to us."

"The staff is adequate," the tall rabbit put in, "if only they would all work to their potential."

"I am sure that will not be a problem with Miss Stone," Mister West said. "Welcome to Fortescue Hall."

"Thank you, sir." That felt like a dismissal, and indeed the elderly badger looked down at a sheaf of papers on his desk. But Ellie felt emboldened to ask one more question. "Sir, if I may?"

He peered up at her through his spectacles. "Miss Davis can answer your questions about the working of the household, I'm certain."

"Yes, sir, but I only wanted to ask—are the books in the library available to the staff as well?"

His expression brightened and his little ears perked up. "You may certainly avail yourself of the library, Miss Stone. Tell me, what kind of books do you like to read?"

"Oh, I like to read whatever I can. I'm interested in people."

"So...travelogues? Memoirs?" He looked keenly at her.

Her ears warmed. "I would read those, certainly, but I was interested in finding your books."

He chuckled. "Flattery is always appreciated, but I don't imagine you have a great interest in archaeology."

"I have some interest, but I wouldn't know where to start." She cleared her throat. "Until now."

"So what do you prefer to read? What have you been reading?"

"Oh, er..." She stopped herself from looking at Miss Davis, whose disapproval of this whole conversation radiated out from her. "I like police novels. Mysteries and the like."

Miss Davis made a short cluck, but restrained herself to that reproval. Mister West, though, sat up straighter. "Indeed," he said. "A love of mysteries indicates a curious mind."

"I am sure it will be of great use to Miss Stone in the kitchen," Miss Davis said firmly.

"Of course, of course." Mister West smiled. "I look forward to seeing you in the library, Miss Stone. You will find my books near the door, and the mysteries in the back corner."

"Thank you, sir." She curtseyed.

"No need for those formalities," Mister West said, but he looked pleased.

Miss Davis waited until they were around the bend and back in the Front Hall before speaking. "Do you really enjoy reading?" she asked. "Or was that to curry favour?"

"I do, honestly," Ellie said. "In my time off, I do hope to read some of his books. At least one."

Miss Davis sniffed again. "What you do on your own time is your own business."

They walked back through the entry hall, Miss Davis at a brisker pace, and this time she walked past the stair, across the hall they'd come in by, and through another door that led to a large dining room. The polished wooden table was currently bare, but had room for at least ten settings (Ellie counted in her head: Mister West, his sister and her husband, their three children plus at least one spouse, two grandchildren—unless one of the spouses had been lost in the war, which might be possible if the children were grown), and the china cabinets were larger than Ellie had seen in any house she'd worked in. The cabinets themselves looked elegant, but not exceedingly so, at least as far as Ellie could judge.

From the dining room, they walked through the narrow servery, where the servants would take dishes from the cooks to bring out to the family in the dining room, and from the servery Miss Davis led Ellie into into the kitchen.

Ellie had expected a large kitchen, but this room was only about as large as Mister West's study. On one side stood the oven, with a six-burner hob atop it; across from the servery door stretched a long wooden counter, and to the left, another counter and the sink and drying rack. At the counter stood a tall skinny fox in a white apron, with a chef's hat covering his ears. "Lorna!" he called, brandishing a middle-sized knife. "Where are those parsnips?"

He spoke with a French accent, but a light one. "Mister LeFou," Miss Davis said. "Your new assistant cook is here."

A short wildcat clutching a bunch of parsnips appeared from a door behind the counter just as the fox turned. He studied Ellie for a moment and then called over his shoulder, "Eggs."

The cat—Lorna—deposited the parsnips on the counter and disappeared back through the door. "I am Laurent LeFou," the fox announced to Ellie. "You are here to learn from me."

"Er, yes," Ellie said.

"Then I must know how much you know." Lorna reappeared and set a basket of eggs on the counter. LeFou, without looking at them, stepped aside and nodded to the basket behind him. "Make an omelette. Lorna! Butter and pan." He did not look away from Ellie the whole time. "You will find whatever else you need in the pantry."

The bobcat hurried to one of the cupboards and brought out a small iron pan and a metal spatula, and then scurried over to the large refrigerator sitting against a wall and took a square of butter on a plate out of it. She set the pan on the stove and the butter next to the eggs, and then walked back over to stand next to the refrigerator, paws clasped together in front of her.

"Er," Ellie said. "Hello. I'm Ellie Stone. It's a pleasure to meet you."

"Yes," LeFou said. "Make the omelette, if you please."

Ellie was not accustomed to making food in front of three people who were just watching her, not contributing to the making of the dinner. And she hadn't made an omelette in weeks, as the Hathaways did not in general take eggs for breakfast unless they had a guest. But she knew how to do it—she thought—and so she asked for a bowl, which Lorna provided, and cracked two eggs into it. "For how many people am I making this omelette?" she asked.

LeFou considered for a moment and then said, "For the people in this room."

For four, that meant eight eggs. She cracked them into the bowl and then went to the pantry to find spices. Her nose led her to a block of cheese; should she add cheese? She took some, added a few herbs she found, and mixed them together in the bowl. Her paws shook, feeling the weight of the people watching her. And then she thought about Abby, the rabbit's soft, steady voice, telling her that she was amazing and could cook anything. Her paws steadied, and Abby's imaginary presence blocked out the other people watching her, at least a little.

After melting the butter in the pan, she poured the egg mixture into it, and a few moments later, she turned the omelette from the pan out onto a plate that Lorna provided. She presented it to LeFou, who took the plate in one dark-furred paw. He took one sniff, then stepped to the side and slid the omelette off the plate and into the bin.

Miss Davis uttered a low cry. Ellie stifled a gasp, Abby's presence dissipating. "You didn't even taste it," she said.

"I did not have to," LeFou said. "I watched you prepare it. You added too much pepper and not enough cheese, just to begin with. I know what it would have tasted like. I know what I can teach you."

"Someone could have eaten that," Miss Davis protested.

"Not from my kitchen," the fox sniffed. "Now, we are preparing supper. I will assign you the potatoes au gratin. Do not worry; I will guide you through so that it is presentable to the family."

* * *

Miss Davis led her out of the kitchen into the servants' corridor, where she delivered some sharp words about LeFou. A parlour-maid by the name of Portia, a chatty Asian otter, happened to be in the hallway, and Miss Davis instructed her to take Ellie up to the second floor and the room she would be sharing with Miss Davis's daughter Lavinia.

It was a short trip up a stair and ten feet along a hallway, but Portia filled it with chatter well enough. When they reached the room, Lavinia lay in her bed drawing in a note-book, but Ellie barely had time to introduce herself and to have Portia point out that she had to go through Ellie and Lavinia's room to get to her own, before she felt she had to hurry back down to the kitchen.

Ellie had made what she'd thought of as potatoes au gratin before, but LeFou had her make a cheese sauce from butter, cheese, and cream, seasoned lightly with salt and thyme. The cheeses had to be grated and then combined with the cream, the potatoes sliced perfectly thinly, the spices in the right proportion. The last time she'd made it, she had sliced the potatoes and then sprinkled cheese over them and put them in the oven. Now she spent an hour getting the potatoes sliced to the right thickness on the mandolin and the cheese grated properly. There were two kinds of cheese, a softer gruyere and a hard fragrant cheese that LeFou called "Asiago," but which she'd never encountered before, and she had to get the propor-tions of the two cheeses correct.

When LeFou came to inspect her potato slices, he picked one up in his fingers. "Is this what you wish to present to the family?" he asked.

"They're done on the mandolin," Ellie replied. "They're all the same size, as you asked."

He turned the slice over in his fingers. "They are not. Some are smaller around, some are larger."

"Potatoes aren't the same size around the whole way," Ellie said. "I can't help that."

"If you slice potatoes on a diagonal, they will be more consistent and fewer will need to be discarded. Set aside the smaller ones; we will use them for the staff dish." And with that he went back to his main course.

Ellie prepared two dishes, one for the family and one for the staff, and put them into the oven, then helped Lorna with the cat's work until it was time for her potatoes to come out, about twenty minutes before supper.

These last twenty minutes were frantic in any kitchen, and Fortescue was no exception. In Ellie's current position, the cook took charge of the main dish and primary side, and left Ellie to the other sides and the bread and butter and such. Here, though, LeFou snapped constantly at Ellie and Lorna, making sure everything was ready before they took it out to the servery, a barrage of "How many slices of bread are there?" and "How long have the potatoes been out? They must not be too hot," and "Arrange the vegetables more pleasingly." Finally, at seven twenty-eight, the dishes were all ready, and LeFou, Ellie, and Lorna brought them out to the servery where Portia was waiting.

Ellie and Lorna set their dishes on the sideboard, but LeFou kept his in his paws and brought it out to the table. Portia followed with the potatoes and the green beans Lorna had prepared, but LeFou announced the dinner. "Oven-roasted pullet with rosemary," he said, and then, when Portia set the other dishes down, "Green beans, and potatoes prepared by Miss Stone."

Through the servery window, Ellie could see the family, and she presumed that as long as the lights remained down in the servery, they wouldn't be able to see her. (This belief was affirmed a moment later when Portia hurried back to the servery and whispered, "Don't turn the lights on!") Mister West sat at the head of the table, wearing the same neat suit and bowtie that he'd been wearing when Ellie had seen him earlier. He looked up when LeFou presented the potatoes and asked, "Are those potatoes au gratin?"

The cook sniffed. "I would not call them that," he said, and bowed stiffly. "Please enjoy your meal."

He walked back to the servery and immediately to the kitchen. Ellie turned to follow, but that was when Portia hurried back in with the admonition about the lights, and whispered to her, "You needn't go back if he doesn't call you. Come on, I'll show you the family."

LeFou was not, in fact, calling for Ellie, so the weasel stayed next to Portia, with whom she felt very at home: another mustelid around her size with the same vibrant energy. "There," Portia said, "facing us, at the head of the table, that's Mister West—"

"I've met him," Ellie said. "I don't know any of the others, but that must be his sister and her husband?"

To Mister West's right sat two older badgers, a lady in a fancy green dress with a gold brooch at her throat and gold bracelets on either arm, and a fellow in a suit that was not as neatly worn as Mister West's: the tie was looser, the jacket askew, and Ellie noticed a stain on one sleeve. Next to him rested a wooden walking stick. "Yes," Portia said. "That's Callie and James MacTavish. She's a battleaxe and he's mostly harmless, but his paws will wander, if you know what I mean."

Ellie did. James wore a broad smile as he tucked into the pullet, and he did look like someone not quite used to the manners of a grand house. He tore meat off the bone with his fork and shoved it between his teeth, while his wife cut each piece of pullet primly and chewed with her mouth firmly closed. "And then across from them are two of their children?"

"The fellow is Finley," Portia said, indicating a handsome badger in a blue suit jacket and green bowtie over a pressed white shirt. He looked like he'd inherited his manners from his mother. "He works at a bank in London. And that's Bonnie, she's a widow and Callie's been trying to arrange meetings with other lords in the area." Bonnie wore a plain shirt—not a dress—and her fur was not as neatly kept as her brother's. She had a distracted air as she ate, as though the conversation around her was a river and she was sitting on a small island in the midst of it.

"How sad," Ellie said.

"Her husband died in the war," Portia said. "The Royal Army sent medals back, but she keeps them locked in her room under the bed. She's not even forty yet, so she could marry again, but she doesn't seem interested in any of the fellows her mother brings around. I don't blame her."

Ellie left sad Bonnie and looked at the youngest badgers, one next to James and the other next to Bonnie. The one next to Bonnie wore a military shirt, she thought, and had leaned a cane on the table. Behind him stood an English otter in a smart suit and tie. Across from him, his brother (she presumed) wore a casual grey shirt, rumpled and also bearing a stain on the sleeve. "And those are the grandchildren?"

"Teddy's the military one," Portia said. "Hurt his leg in the war. Not the big war, the one over in Korea. Todd was too young to go, just sixteen when they stopped sending people over."

"Is that why Teddy has a servant and nobody else does?"

Portia nodded. "But he wasn't assigned by the army or anything. That's Devon. He was in Teddy's regiment during the war and he says Teddy saved his life."

"'He says,'" Ellie repeated. "You don't believe him?"

"Well, I wasn't there, was I?" Portia flashed her a smile. "I suppose it's very likely true. I can only think of one other reason one fellow would be so devoted to another, and Devon has a girlfriend, so that reason is probably out." She winked at Ellie.

Ellie felt a little queasy, the way she did anytime someone referenced same-sex relationships around her. If she said the wrong thing, she feared, someone would know about her and Abby. If she let it go without speaking, or if she condemned it too strongly, or allowed as how it was a modern thing, any of those might lead to her being found out. So she nodded and changed the subject. "And they're Bonnie's children?"

"Oh no, they're Ian and Catherine's. They're not here. On holiday for the summer, they said, but I happened to see a card they sent to Todd and it was postmarked from Edinburgh, and that just happens to be where Catherine's family lives, so…"

"So…they're on holiday with family?"

"People don't go on holiday to where they live. Your family, they're in, what, Monte Carlo is it?"

"Monaco."

"There you are. They didn't go on holiday to Birmingham, did they?"

"Then…" Ellie frowned. "They went to see family, but they didn't want anyone to know?"

Portia nodded, pleased. "Exactly! Oh, hush a moment."

Callie had raised her voice. "I do not understand why you persist in refusing," she snapped across the table.

Finley, apparently the target of her remark, avoided her gaze. His voice was low, but the table had gone quiet and Ellie heard him clearly. "I can't simply grant him a position, Mother. There are rules—"

"Oh, poppycock," she said. "Are you not manager of an entire branch?"

"Department," he corrected her.

"Grandma," Todd said, "It's all right. I don't want—"

"I won't have you sitting around here all day like a vagabond," she said.

("Don't vagabonds move around quite a bit?" Ellie whispered.

"Shh," Portia said, but giggled.)

"The boy can sit around," James said. "Don't force him into a job he doesn't want."

"Of course you would say that." Callie glared at her husband, and he turned an apologetic glance at Todd and then went back to eating his supper.

Finley set down his fork. "I can't simply hire someone. Hiring is overseen by a different department."

"Bryce Halloran got his nephew a job in his bank," Callie said.

Finley took in a deep breath, the kind of breath one takes in when one has heard the same argument repeated over and over, and Mister West jumped in. "Maybe you should ask Bryce Halloran to get Todd a job," he said with a smile.

"Charles, you're not helping," Callie said.

"I told you, Mother, Bryce is president of the Midlands Bank. I'm a department head."

"So you don't have any power whatsoever," she said.

"As I told you," he said patiently, and then Bonnie put a paw on his arm, and he paused to look at her.

"Don't banks offer a sort of learning position?" Bonnie asked. Her voice was low and clear, and of all the people at the table she hadn't seen before, Ellie liked her the best. She had been following the conversation intelligently and broke in only now, when she had something to say.

Everyone turned to Finley. "Er, yes," he said, a little surprised. "We can take an intern who's interested in a career in banking."

"That's all I've been asking you to do," Callie said. "Why did that take three arguments to get to?"

"It's not a paid position," Finley said. "It's just for someone to get accustomed to the bank. It can lead to a paid position, but usually not for six months or a year."

The table now turned their attention to Callie. Ellie saw

Mister West's expression most clearly and was surprised to see what she thought might be sadness there. He was all the way across a room, and badgers were sometimes harder to read than other people, but he felt sad to Ellie all the same.

"That's fine," Callie said. "What's important is the boy has something to occupy him."

Teddy pushed himself back from the table and stood up so abruptly his chair almost fell backwards. Devon caught it and pulled it all the way back as the young badger seized his cane and took a step back from the table. "You're not even his mother," he said. "Why can't you leave anything alone?"

Callie didn't respond immediately, but James said, "Don't work yourself up, Teddy old fellow."

"If his mother would take charge of him," Callie said coldly, "then there would be no need for me to. I'm only trying to help the boy."

"Help someone who wants it, why don't you?" Teddy smacked his cane against the table with a rap that made everyone jump—Ellie and Portia included—and then turned and stomped off out of the dining room.

But that wasn't the end of it. Todd jumped up to run after him, and stopped him just outside the doorway, still in Ellie and Portia's view. They couldn't hear what was said, because Callie was saying something about the war having done damage and Bonnie retorting sharply, but they both saw Todd tug on Teddy's sleeve and say something, and then saw Teddy shove his brother hard into a wall.

Todd stayed there while Teddy walked away and Devon followed him, and then the young badger brushed his shirt, put on a smile, and walked back into the dining room. "I'll give him some time to cool off," he said to the questioning silence.

"Portia!" Callie called, and as Portia hurried out, Ellie returned to the kitchen.

CHAPTER 3
FORTESCUE HALL

My dearest Abby,

I've arrived safely at Fortescue Hall. I promised to write as soon as I got here, and so I'm doing that now, even though Portia keeps nattering on at me.

Portia is an Asian otter, and she's been here in the room I'm sharing with Lavinia for almost an hour. She has to pass through our room on the way to her room, but she says there's nobody else in her room and she wants to visit with us, so she's sat here. Lavinia's drawing in her pad and I'm very pointedly writing, but that doesn't stop Portia from telling us whatever comes into her head and asking us questions when she can't think of anything else. She asked my favorite kind of bread, and when I said, "rye," she said, "how curious," and went off for twenty minutes about someone she knew who'd made rye bread, or maybe wanted to make rye bread because she'd heard about it. It all goes by so fast.

But she's a kind person, as is Lavinia—Lavinia is Miss Davis's daughter, and Miss Davis thinks she's flighty, but I think she's interesting and creative. Oh dear, I feel I should start with telling you about all the people I've met today. I'll do that, and maybe it will help me keep them straight in my head as well. And I have to tell you about what LeFou did—he's the chef, and he's—well, I'll get to him presently. I've never felt so small, and for no reason!

Miss Davis is a rabbit, Fortescue Hall's head of staff. She rules the roost, and I know all the heads we've known have been strict, but I feel Miss Davis would bring them all in line. She met me off the train and walked me to the Hall and laid down all the rules as we walked. I fear we won't be able to arrange a day off in my month here, and I don't think I will be allowed a visitor. I'm sorry, old soul, but I'll ask again when I've my feet under me. The good news is that I have a ready-made excuse to put off Sergeant Cooke for another month, the poor fellow. He wanted me to visit when he found out I wasn't going on holiday with the Hathaways, as you can imagine. Perhaps I can take this month to really think through your advice and put it into action when I'm back in Widden's Crossing.

But I must tell you about the hall! It quite deserves its own letter. It's almost more a palace. There are Wings, and one of the wings is closed for repairs, and it's so grand inside—not the wing closed for repairs, I mean, but the parts I was allowed into—with dark wood trim and marble floors, at least in the main hall, which I got to glimpse quickly. The floors in the rest of the house are wood, which Portia says she's kept busy from sunup to sundown dusting and polishing, she and the other two housemaids.

I wish you could see it! There's a sun room Miss Davis is very proud of, and as it was early afternoon still, the family had not occupied it yet, so we were permitted to walk in. The glass has gold trim around it, looking out onto the gardens, and the chairs are a light birch wood with gold and red cushions and covers. When the setting sun shines in, it must be truly lovely.

This room I'm in now, on the second story, is not so nice. The main house was built in the 1600s and renovated a century ago, but I think they may have passed over the servants' quarters in the renovation. The walls are cold stone, but we have warm blankets and a wool rug, and there's a fireplace for winter. Lavinia says it stays surprisingly warm with just a small fire, even in winter.

Right. The family. I thought I would first meet the staff, but Miss Davis told me that Mister West, he's the head of house, he wants to meet all new staff immediately. So we saw him in his study, which is the size of the dining room at the St. Clair's, all dark wood and books and about twenty clay and stone statues and things around the room that I didn't look too closely at. He's an archaeologist, Miss Davis told me, someone who digs up old cities to see what we can learn about the people who lived there. He's written several books, some of which were apparently very popular.

Mister West is an old badger, but he has a smile that put me at ease quickly. He asked a little about myself, told me the rules of the house, and was about to dismiss us when I asked if any of his books were available to read for the staff. He told me that staff were welcome to use the library in their off hours, and that a complete collection of his books was held there, "as well as many others that might be of interest." His eyes twinkled when he said that, I promise you, Abby.

That was quite nice, but as we left, Miss Davis didn't waste any time in telling me that Mister West gets along with everyone, and I shouldn't expect that I would be singled out for favorable treatment. I said, "No'm," very properly, because I didn't want her to think I'd been putting on airs. And in any case, she said, Mister West would be leaving in two or three weeks to supervise a dig he'd been asked to consult on, so he wouldn't be here the whole time. I was surprised at this, because I thought he was retired, but she explained that while he didn't stay away for months or years anymore, he did often help colleagues set up digs, or consult on particularly interesting finds.

I didn't meet any of the rest of the family until dinner, which I will tell you about presently, but I met, let me see, four other staff members. Not including Lavinia, who is sharing this room with me, and whom I've already told you about.

There was William, a hedgehog, who seems very shy and quiet and wouldn't meet my eyes at all. "He's a bit odd," Miss Davis said, right in front of him, "but you can ask him where anything in the house is and he'll tell you in a second. And don't put anything back not in its place."

I asked if that would upset him, because he reminded me a little of Bess, you remember her, the little girl next door at the St. Clair's, and Miss Davis said that of course it would, but in a well-run household, things should be in their place anyway, and then she looked at me as though I were some kind of convicted misplaced-items criminal.

By contrast, Portia made up for all the words William didn't say, and then some. She clasped my paw, said how nice it was to have another mustelid on the staff, immediately asked if I were married, and when I said no, asked if I were seeing anyone. Then she told me, before I'd even asked, that William wasn't seeing anyone, "But have you met him? You won't be interested in him," and said that Devon, who is the valet of one of the family, was around my age—without having asked me my age—but that it was no use going for him, because he was seeing a young lady from the grocer's and it seemed quite serious. I asked if that was Georgette the badger, and Portia said it was, and how delightful, and did I know her?

At this point, Miss Davis stepped in and said that was quite enough. I think it was the first chance she had to step in, honestly, because even when I broke in to ask about Georgette, Portia barely paused to let me talk. But she seems delightful and as I said, she is sitting here on Lavinia's bed chattering as I write. She told me about all the family members over dinner.

Then I went into the lovely kitchen, rather large, with two ovens and a refrigerator. That's where I met the chef, Laurent LeFou. He's a tall French fox and, well, I should tell you what he did, that'll be easier.

He speaks excellent English, with just a little French touch to it, but the English accent he speaks is very schoolroom, you know. It's not West Country, nor Oxford, nor any of the London accents I know. But anyway, the first thing he said was, "Make an omelette."

So I did—and I imagined you there with me, supporting me—and he didn't even taste it, he just picked up the plate and dumped the omelette into the bin! He told me that the omelette was too dry and that I had added too much pepper and not enough cheese. He said he would never serve something like that. Abby, I hid it from everyone else, but I felt tears in my eyes.

And then he put his paw on my shoulder and he said that it was no less than he'd expected and he could definitely teach me. I happened to see Lorna's muzzle when he said that, and it twisted up angrily, though I don't know whether it was from the touch or what he said. Perhaps he is more spiteful toward her. Or it could be that she was jealous of the attention? It could be that they are a couple.

That thought was in my head as we left the kitchen, and I asked Miss Davis on the way up to my room, but I couldn't even get the whole question out. She interrupted me to say, "That LeFou is a disgrace to any proper kitchen. Yes, he is a talented chef, but kitchen staff are about more than the food that comes out of them. He is the blackest mark on this household's otherwise excellent—or at least very satisfactory—staff."

(I have quoted her here, and the words may not be exactly right, but I believe they are, because the force with which they were delivered made a great impression on me. And I confess I was still upset at him throwing out the omelette.)

Portia says that he's always been perfectly lovely to her, but that everyone complains about him to her. She said—well, I don't remember all of them, but she said that Callie and James—Callie is Mister West's sister, and they are the parents or grandparents of everyone else in the family who lives here, Mister West being a bachelor. Callie and James tolerate him for their brother's sake, but they've tried to have him dismissed twice. And then—well, bother, old soul, this letter is so long already. I'll tell you more about the family in the next one. They had a row at dinner and it was rather interesting. I know, it's terrible of me to say 'it's rather interesting' and then not give you details, but this way you'll look forward to my next letter.

I hope this finds you well, and don't worry about me. I'll be fine, even if it will be an interesting month here. Wish me luck. If all goes well, I'll feel much better about putting my name in when your Mrs. Deerwood retires next year. Imagine being able to be in the same household again! To be able to see you every night again—oh, it makes my paws shake. I shall put the pen down now, but not those dreams.

Love,

Ellie

CHAPTER 4
THE PARLOUR

"That's quite a letter," Portia said as Ellie finished writing. "Who did you say you're writing to?"

"Just my friend," Ellie said, turning the letter over as Portia craned her neck to see. "We were in service together."

"And you still write to her? I can't imagine. I've been in service for years and I don't keep in touch with anyone."

"Well," Lavinia said dreamily from her bed, lying on her back, "Ellie is a creative person and you're not."

The small otter jumped down and stood to her full height, about four and a half feet. "What do you mean? She's just writing a letter."

"Writing is one of the creative arts."

"But she's not making up a novel. She's just writing down—things that happened. News."

"And feelings, perhaps." Lavinia seemed entirely unruffled by Portia's indignance.

Ellie, feeling rather warm at being the subject of discussion, said, "We've just got into the habit of writing. It's nice to have a friend to write to. It takes me out of myself a little."

"There, you see?" Lavinia said. "Creativity. Meditative."

"Oh!" Portia exclaimed. "I've got to get to bed anyway." And she flounced out into her room with a huff and closed the door behind her.

Ellie stared after her. "You mustn't mind her," Lavinia said from her bed. "She desperately wants to know everything that goes on."

"Oh, I've known people like her." Ellie folded the letter carefully and slid it into the drawer of the little desk, then crossed to lie down on her own bed. The desk—small but well-crafted, with faded painted flowers around the border, probably outgrown from one of the children's rooms or from one of the older women who'd passed away—was shared between the two of them, but already she trusted Lavinia not to look at the letter.

"There's one in every staff, my mother tells me."

Ellie turned onto her side, resting on one elbow. Lavinia's fur was a lighter brown than Portia's, and she had much more roundness about her than either Portia or Ellie, which was another reason she didn't remind Ellie of Abby. The dreaminess was similar, but that was all. She more resembled her mother in all the ways she didn't resemble Abby. "How did you end up so different from your mother?"

Lavinia laughed softly. "She's told you about me, I suppose."

"Er...yes, she did."

"Mind you don't take after any of my bad habits."

"Oh," Ellie said, frowning. "I—I'm sure I don't know what you're talking about."

Lavinia waved at the ceiling. "There's an empty servant's room just down the hall. But she puts new staff in with me. Hoping I'll learn from dedicated servants, you see."

"I'm sure..." Ellie paused, thinking about whether to reveal that Miss Davis had asked her to set Lavinia right. Even before meeting Lavinia, Ellie wondered what she could do to help someone appreciate a life of service more, but now, with this self-assured rabbit before her, the request seemed even more hopeless.

"Trust me," Lavinia said. "She's told me as much. And here I am, still unchanged. I'm quite pleased with my life, and I'm sure your example won't make any more difference than the three before you."

"I think," Ellie replied after a moment, "that being happy with one's life is just about the most important thing there is."

She thought Lavinia had forgotten her original question, but the rabbit spoke again a moment later. "Mother is so devoted to her work, and she wanted me to be too, but I found friends in brushes and fulfillment in dance. It never seemed to me that her work brought her much happiness, not what my paintings brought me. I wished she could find joy in them, but alas." She lay her arm over her forehead for all the world like a tragic heroine. "Twas not to be."

"I'm sorry," Ellie said.

"Mothers and daughters, 'twas ever thus." Lavinia turned and peeked below her arm out at Ellie.

Ellie smiled. "I'd love to see some of your drawings, if you feel like showing them."

The rabbit's eyes widened. "Really? If you're interested, then...yes. I'll pick out the ones I like best." She continued to look at Ellie. "I wager someone who writes letters also reads."

"I do." Ellie looked away for a moment, because Lavinia seemed like someone who would want her to read Bronte and Austen. But she couldn't lie about what she'd read, because what if Lavinia had also read them and wanted to talk about them? "Police novels are my favorite, I'm afraid."

"That's charming. I don't think I know anyone else who reads that sort of thing."

"I like the mystery parts," Ellie said.

Lavinia considered this. "I think I would find the mystery quite taxing. Crime is so...sad. What is it that attracts you to it?"

"Oh," Ellie said, "I don't know exactly. I suppose that it's... well, people who commit crime, especially something like murder, well, it must be a very extreme thing, mustn't it? Either a normal person driven to extreme measures, or an unusually extreme person. I think those are interesting."

"I see." Lavinia turned her head back to stare at the ceiling. "Rather like when I find an interesting tree bent into an unusual shape, I suppose."

"Rather," Ellie said.

"All right. That makes sense to me." She paused. "Have you ever witnessed a murder?"

"Well." Ellie hesitated. "I've been in a house where there was a murder. And I was called to another one."

"You were *called*? So you're a detective of sorts."

"Oh no," she hurried to say. "But the sergeant who handled the first case, he likes me, and so he asked if I would—"

"He likes you?" Lavinia interrupted. "Will you be writing him a letter as well, or only if there's a murder?"

Ellie paused. "I don't expect there will be a murder..."

"Then he likes you more than you like him. I see." Lavinia paused. "You don't think anyone in this house is capable of committing a murder?"

"Oh," Ellie said, "if the circumstances were right, I suppose anyone could. I don't know them well enough. I don't think you could, though."

Lavinia half-turned toward her with an amused look. "You barely know me."

"You just don't seem like the sort to get your ire up—you don't care enough about anything but your art. And if someone took one of your paintings, you could paint another, couldn't you?"

"What if someone threatened to stop my art altogether?" Lavinia asked quietly.

Ellie thought about it. "I don't know," she said. "Would you kill them then?"

There were several seconds of silence, and then Lavinia said, "Well, good night. You can leave the fire; it'll burn down on its own." And with that, she rolled over to face away from Ellie.

* * *

Portia came and woke Lavinia a little after sunrise. "Come on," she chirped, last night's huff forgotten. "Lavinia, you've rooms to turn down, and Ellie, you're to report to the kitchen."

"Yes, of course." Ellie had been up and was halfway dressed already.

Lavinia yawned and sat up. Ellie finished dressing and made her way down to the kitchen, where she found only LeFou.

"Punctuality is admirable, at least," he said. "Are you able to make toast without burning it?"

"Of course," Ellie said. "I can make toast and, cr—crumpets." She'd been about to say "croissants," which she had made, but she felt that the scorn a nasty French fox would direct at her croissants, even hypothetical ones, would be intolerable. "And sausages."

He snorted. "Only the toast for now. I will occupy myself with the rest. When Lorna arrives, hoping that is not after breakfast has been served, she will prepare the sausages. She knows how I like them done."

Finley appeared before Lorna did, dressed in a smart blue suit with a bright yellow pocket square. He held a fashionable trilby hat in one paw. "Morning, LeFou," he said. "Oh, er—hallo, Miss Stein."

"Stone, sir," Ellie corrected him.

"Quite." He walked over to the bread Ellie was slicing for

toast and took two large pieces of it in his free paw, then set his hat between his ears. "Cheers," he said, and left the kitchen.

Lorna did in fact appear before breakfast, just as Ellie was finishing the last of the toast—nearly an entire loaf of bread sliced up for it, all but the ends. The cat's fur looked unkempt and her apron was askew, as though she'd dressed in a hurry, but Ellie caught a whiff of soap, so she'd had time to wash. The cat met Ellie's eye and then mumbled, "G'morning, sir," to LeFou and went to get the sausages from the pantry.

"Miss Stone is making the toast today," LeFou informed her. "Show her where the butter and jam are kept."

"Yessir," Lorna said. She dropped the sausages next to the stove and fetched a glass jar of jam and a paper-wrapped square of butter from the pantry and refrigerator.

Ellie took them from her. "Thank you," she said.

LeFou examined her toast. "It is adequate," he sniffed. "Better than Lorna does."

Lorna's shoulders hunched, but she didn't give any sign that she'd heard. Ellie remembered, though, and when LeFou took the eggs and sausages out, Ellie went to stand next to the cat, who was cleaning the pan and wooden fork. "He didn't have to say that," she said.

"It's all right," Lorna whispered. "I know I'm not very good."

"You are, though," Ellie said. "And his job should be to teach you to be better."

"No," the cat said, "he's teaching *you*. He tolerates me."

He came back then, and they finished up breakfast. But Ellie wondered how long Lorna had been made to feel small and incompetent. How long could someone take that kind of abuse? What would it do to them?

When breakfast had been served, and Portia had cleared the dishes, LeFou left Ellie and Lorna to do the washing-up. Ellie took the opportunity to try to cheer up the cat. "I think you're doing rather well," she said.

Lorna didn't respond, only took the next plate and cleaned it mechanically. "Do you want to be a cook in your own kitchen one day?" Ellie continued, determined to make some sort of connection with the cat.

"Oh no," Lorna said. "I'm not the sort who could run a kitchen."

"I think you might be." Ellie dried the plates. "You just need the confidence to do it."

Lorna shook her head. "I'd make a mess of it like I do everything else."

"Now, you shouldn't talk like that. Listen. I'm going to practice that omelette, and I'd like you to help. Can I use the eggs in the pantry?"

The cat's eyes got wide, and she nearly dropped the plate. "I don't know," she said. "He keeps tally of everything."

"He let me use eight eggs yesterday and he threw them into the bin."

"But that was his decision." Lorna set the plate on the drying rack. "I really don't know. You should ask him."

"Right," Ellie said. "I'll ask him then. You stay here to help me when I come back. Where would I find him?"

"If he's not in his quarters, then he's likely somewhere else in the house," Lorna said.

Ellie saw it wasn't going to be any use talking further to her, so she left to find LeFou on her own.

The family had scattered from the dining room, and most of the staff as well. Ellie first walked out the back of the kitchen to the cook's quarters, but LeFou was not there. She ventured back into the house proper.

On her way past the library, it occurred to her that there might be a book about French sauces that she could read in her room at night to speed up her learning. And besides, she was eager to see the books that might be available to her. So she stepped into the empty room and looked around—only to find that it wasn't empty after all. A badger sat in a plush armchair to the right of the door, invisible to anyone looking in from the hallway. She wore a blue dress, bunched up around her knees by the book she held in her lap. Above her, a window let in plenty of light to read, and the glass of water on the table beside her sparkled with sun.

She noticed Ellie a moment after Ellie recognized Bonnie. With a start, she slammed the book shut and pushed it down beside her leg. "What are you doing in here?" she snapped.

"I—I'm sorry, Mrs. Bonnie," Ellie said. "I was looking for Mister LeFou."

"As you can see, he's not here, just as anyone with sense would have expected. So you may continue your search elsewhere."

"I'm sorry, ma'am." Ellie attempted a curtsy, feeling very flushed with embarrassment at the unintentional intrusion she'd made, even if she wasn't entirely clear on what that was. The staff were allowed the run of the house, she'd been told that specifically. "I don't know where he's likely to be."

Bonnie peered at her. "Oh. You're that new weasel. I thought you were Portia for a moment. Well, I'm afraid I can't help you. I stay away from that fox as much as I can. I enjoy his food, but it isn't worth all the rest of what he brings."

"Thank you, ma'am," Ellie said. "I'll be on my way, then. And thank you for saying you liked my potatoes."

But before she'd taken two steps, Bonnie stopped her. "I did like them. What's your name again? I remember Stone, but not the first name."

"Ellie, ma'am."

"Ellie. Listen, it doesn't do for you too become to familiar with the family here."

This felt like an odd bit of advice; Ellie knew her place. "Ma'am?"

"Oh, you needn't call me 'ma'am,'" Bonnie said crossly.

"That's not what I meant. I just meant that...look, you're here to cook for us. Nobody in our family should ask you to do anything else, that's all I mean."

"I see," Ellie said doubtfully.

"If something happens...you'll know what I mean...you come and see me, and I'll talk to my uncle and we'll put it right. Don't try to take matters into your own paws. And if we're not here, you can trust in Miss Davis. She won't be straight with you, but she'll take care of it."

"Yes'm." Ellie wondered why the warning had to be phrased that way.

She found out, she thought, a few minutes later, as she was making her way from the library to what she thought was the sun room. She'd followed a bright light and the smell of the outdoors around two bends in the corridor but found herself looking into a drawing room that Portia was airing out, with windows that looked onto the garden. The otter said she had no idea where LeFou spent his time when he wasn't in the kitchen, but she often talked to him in the staff's common room behind the kitchen, where they took their meals.

But Ellie had only rounded one corner on her way back there before she encountered Teddy and Devon, Teddy walking slowly with his cane and Devon the otter preceding him.

Devon jumped forward a step as though Ellie were a threat. "What'choo doing here?" he asked, chin out, belligerent.

"Steady, Devon," the badger said. "Miss Stone is new to Fortescue and I'm sure she's just gotten lost."

"Yes, sir, thank you." Ellie curtsied, her fur prickling a little as she remembered the shove Teddy had given his brother. He was dressed in the same military uniform, or at least a similar one. "I was looking for Mr. LeFou, and I—"

She turned to point to the bedroom where Portia had given her directions, but the badger cut her off before she could continue. "That bastard better not be anywhere near here."

His whole demeanor had changed: fist clenched around his cane, eyes glaring. Devon put a paw on the badger's wrist. "Steady, sir," he said.

"He's not," Ellie said hastily. "Portia told me to check the staff room."

The badger—Teddy—relaxed, but slowly, eyes darting to either side as though the fox might jump out of one of the doors. And Ellie recalled now that he'd seemed tense when dinner was being served, although not as tense as he'd been a few minutes ago. She'd thought maybe he was always like that. "Yes," he said. "The staff room. But look in on my great-uncle's study first. For some reason, he enjoys LeFou's company."

"Thank you, sir." Ellie curtsied again. She made to hurry past them, but Devon grabbed her arm.

"Ey," he said. "Sorry about earlier. If you got time later, I could tell you more 'bout how the house runs. Show you 'round maybe."

His eyes gleamed with the implication of the invitation. Ellie didn't want to antagonize him this early into her stay, so she didn't let her disinterest show. "Oh, that would be lovely," she said, "but Mr. LeFou does keep me busy in the kitchen."

"Only mealtimes," Devon said, and was going to say more, but Teddy snapped his fingers, and the otter jumped. "Ah, right. Well, if it happens to work out..." And then he followed Teddy on down the hall.

Wasn't he supposed to be seeing Georgette? Certainly Ellie had known young fellows happy to see one girl by day and one by night, or even one for each day of the week. Perhaps Devon was one of those. She put it out of her mind and went on to Mister West's study.

The door was closed, but the murmur of voices came through. Ellie, without really thinking about it, put her ear to the door.

"His name is Parker," LeFou was saying. "I believe he is a

hedgehog. I do not know more than that. Portia saw him there, but she did not understand what it means."

Mister West's deep baritone answered. "I've suspected for some time, of course."

"So what are you going to do about it?"

"Do? What should I do?"

Ellie took her ear from the door, embarrassed, and then knocked.

The murmurs stopped. Mister West's voice called, "Who is it?"

"It's Ellie Stone, sir," she called. "I am looking for Mr. LeFou. Your grand-nephew said he might be here."

No reply came to that, but a moment later, the door opened, and Ellie looked up into the russet and white muzzle of LeFou. "Yes?" he snapped. "What is it?"

"I wanted to practice my omelette," Ellie stammered. "But I needed eggs."

"Lorna knows where the eggs are." He started to close the door.

"I—may I use as many as I need?"

His ears flattened. He frowned. "Of course," he said.

"Thank you for coming to ask permission," Mister West called from behind her.

LeFou flicked his ears back. "Yes," he said. "Well done. William will fetch eggs for breakfast in the morning. The others are for you to use. And if you wish to practice your toast as well, you may use as much of the bread as you wish. I would advise it."

"Thank you, sir." Ellie nodded her head as the door closed in her face.

* * *

On her way back to the kitchen, Ellie returned via the Front Hall, where several doors stood open (though the library door was now closed). From one of them, a deep, cheery voice followed her. "Ho there, girl!"

She stopped and retraced her steps, peering into one door and then another until she looked in on a parlour where James MacTavish reclined in a chair. "Yes, you," he said as she met his eyes. "Stop here a moment, will you?"

There wasn't a question of saying no, not to one of the family. So Ellie stepped into the parlour and stood just inside the doorway.

The badger smiled at her and spoke with a burr to his deep voice. "You're Miss Stone, is that right?" Without waiting for more than a nod, he went on. "I'm James MacTavish. I'm here by right of having married Callie West, that's Charles's sister, and Charles has been nice enough to invite our brood here to live. I suppose it's better than rattling around in an empty house, wouldn't you think?"

"I suppose," Ellie said politely. The old badger's plush armchair sat next to the fireplace, in front of an open window that let in the summer air. Next to it rested his walking-stick, a thick wood staff nearly Ellie's height with a smooth-worn badger's head for a handle. Over the fireplace, a mirror reflected the rest of the dark wood room trimmed with gold leaf in small, tasteful places. A large portrait of a badger—likely Mister West's father, as she didn't recognize him—stared at the door where Ellie had come in, and though there was a long couch in front of the fireplace and another chair facing the one James sat in, he did not offer her a seat.

"Now you're here while the Hardaways are in Monaco, is that right?"

"The Hathaways, sir, yes."

"Of course, of course." He shifted in his chair. "I raced in Monaco, did you know that?"

"No, sir." Ellie knew little about Monaco, but she knew there was a famous race there. "That must have been very exciting."

"It was, it was. Come closer, you don't have to stand all the way over there."

Ellie took a few steps toward him, still a good ten feet from his chair and outstretched paw. He accepted this but kept the paw out. "Motorcars were different then, you know, not so dangerous. I was quite the driver in my day. We went down there, me and Callie, with all the children. Ian was just out of school, I believe, and Bonnie and Finley were on summer break, but old enough they could enjoy it. Let's see, if Ian was twenty, Bonnie would be seventeen and Finley, oh, I don't know, let's say thirteen or fourteen. Ian didn't want to do much with the family anymore, but he did like racing, and Catherine came along, because they were seeing each other already. Teddy wouldn't be born for a few years after that, but you know, it all seemed to happen so fast. I didn't think at the time that that would be our last family vacation together, but..."

He trailed off and stared at the wall to Ellie's right for a moment. She was about to interrupt him when he harrumphed and said, "But Monaco was lovely. It rained once the whole two weeks, I believe. And I came sixth out of fifty cars! I had good reflexes then." He mimed wrestling a car's steering wheel back and forth.

"That's wonderful, sir. To be part of such an historic race."

"Oh, it wasn't in the Grand Prix, heavens no." He beamed at her. "I wasn't that good. It was a qualifying race. They wanted the top three drivers, so I didn't quite make it, you see, but sixth was a jolly good finish. And it was an excuse to have the family in Monaco anyway. We had some divine meals there, and Ian and I sailed over to Marseille one of the days. And the best part is, Callie played cards in the evening and nearly paid for the whole trip. She's a sharp one, that wife of mine."

"I look forward to meeting her, sir," Ellie said.

"Oh, she's about here, somewhere." He looked vaguely out the window. "Likes the gardens this time of year. You know, she tried to teach Ian and Catherine the cards, but they hadn't the patience for it. Hah? Hah?" He turned to her with an expectant smile, but at Ellie's puzzled expression, he shook his head. "Patience is the name of a game one plays with cards," he explained. "By oneself."

"My mother didn't hold with games of chance," Ellie said. "Though I'd like to have learned."

"Oh!" This brightened him considerably. "I have a deck of cards right here. I'd be delighted to show you a thing or two, my dear. Why don't you come over here—"

"James!" The sharp voice came from the doorway. Ellie turned to see Callie standing in the hallway looking in. When she turned, the elderly badger's eyes landed on her. "Oh, it's you, Miss Stone. What are you doing here? Is there nothing to be done in the kitchen?"

"I—"

"And you." She turned her attention to her husband. "Surely you have better ways to occupy your time than bothering this young lady."

"I wasn't bothering her, my dear, was I?" He looked beseechingly at Ellie.

"No, sir, but I was on my way back to the kitchen—"

"The way to the kitchen runs through the parlour, does it?" Callie asked sharply.

"I'll just—"

James cut her off. "Is it any wonder she doesn't want to get back to old LeFou? I thought it wise to show her some good company in this house so she doesn't think it's all..." He mimed chopping. "Fangs and claws."

Callie went still, and the glare she sent her husband's way would have sent Ellie scurrying from the room if it had been aimed at her. "I know what that's supposed to mean."

"What's that, sweetheart?" James asked blandly.

She raised a finger to him. "Just because I know the distinction between family and servant in this house—" She stopped herself. "You do know why Miss Stone is here, don't you?"

James' reaction to that surprised Ellie. He looked away, rubbed his whiskers, and didn't answer.

Obviously, Callie was implying that whatever vacancy Ellie was filling was her husband's fault. She hadn't even realized that there was a vacancy; she'd just thought Mr. West had agreed to take her on for a month. At any rate, Ellie liked James better than Callie, and so rather than flee to the kitchen immediately, she threw him a lifeline so he wouldn't think she suspected. "Oh," she said. "Did Mr. LeFou drive off the last assistant cook?" And then she remembered Teddy's reaction to the mention of the cook, and worked in a little nudge for more information. "Maybe that's why Teddy is so angry with him."

This revived James. "Oh, no, it's nothing to do with that." He shook his head. "They nearly came to blows a month ago, I think it was, over something LeFou said. Would have, too, but for Devon stepping between them. Caught a fist on the shoulder, he did. From Teddy, not LeFou."

"Oh! What did Mr. LeFou say to him?" Ellie asked.

"It's not your concern," Callie said sharply.

"She's working for him. She has a right to know what he's like, dear," James said. "It was something about carrots. That's what was served for dinner."

"Why would Master Teddy get upset about carrots?" Ellie asked.

"It wasn't carrots," Callie snapped. "He said that Teddy appreciated fine tomatoes. All right? Have we finished gossiping like old biddies with nothing better to do? Miss Stone: I believe you know the way back to the kitchen."

Ellie curtseyed and left the room, but she heard James arguing behind her. "Why would he say tomatoes? We hadn't been served tomatoes."

"You know how that boy is," Callie replied, still audible as Ellie walked slowly down the hall. "Now don't let me catch you alone with that girl again."

In the entryway, she nearly ran into Portia, who had clearly been listening but made a show of dusting a vase that sat on a side table in the hall. "You can't just wander about the house," the small otter told Ellie.

"He called me in," Ellie said, "and anyway I was on my way back to the kitchen. I had to ask LeFou about the eggs."

"What about the eggs?" Portia called, but Ellie hurried on and didn't answer.

CHAPTER 5
THE KITCHEN

Ellie made the omelette for herself and Lorna, and this time they did not throw it into the bin but shared it between them and William, who arrived partway through the cooking process and stood silently watching them, a short figure in a neat shirt and trousers with a hedgehog's short, pointed muzzle. When Ellie set down the pepper on the counter, the hedgehog waited a few seconds and then stepped forward and picked it up to put it away in its place.

Nobody had tasted the omelette Ellie'd made the previous day, but she thought this one was better. When she asked William and Lorna how they liked it, William said shyly, "It's good," and Lorna nodded her head.

"But Lorna," Ellie asked, "is it the kind of good that LeFou would approve of?"

Lorna flinched. "Oh, I don't know," she said. "Nothing's good enough for him. Not in here." Then she looked quickly to the door.

"I'll just have to keep getting better," Ellie decided. "And that means I need to know what could improve." The omelette tasted fine to her, but if she were being very critical, it was still a little dry. And the cheese was overwhelming; she might have added too much instead of too little this time. There was room for more herbs, she thought as well. "What I really need to do is taste one of LeFou's omelettes," she said aloud. "Then I'd see what he thinks is so wonderful."

"Oh, they're excellent," Lorna said. "They're creamy and cheesy and...just lovely."

"How is this one different?" Ellie asked.

"Well, it's...it's not as creamy," the wildcat said. "But otherwise it's rather nice."

"I'll try again tomorrow, since we're out of eggs."

"Out of eggs," William repeated. "I'll fetch eggs in the morning."

"Thank you." Ellie smiled at him, but he didn't react, only turned and left the kitchen.

"Don't mind him," Lorna said. "He's shy until he gets to know you better."

"I don't mind, but thank you for telling me." Ellie took the pan and the plates to the sink for the washing up and had just finished when LeFou returned to the kitchen to prepare lunch.

He lifted his nose and then asked Ellie, "How was the omelette this time?"

"Better, I think," she replied, "but I have a good deal to learn."

"You do." He rubbed his chin. "But it is good that you understand that. Perhaps one month will not be entirely wasted. Now come. Lunch is simple, but all the more reason to prepare it well."

* * *

So it went for the next few days. Ellie made her omelette every day, feeling that if she could make it to LeFou's satisfaction, she would really have learned something. She wrote another letter to Abby as she saw more of the different badgers of the

MacTavish family. Callie, the matriarch, made sharp comments about the dress of any of the young ladies on staff, while James jovially defended them, but though they seemed to argue constantly, they were often close by each other. Bonnie remained enigmatic but friendlier than she'd been the day Ellie'd surprised her in the library, and Ellie thought privately that she was the cleverest of the young MacTavishes. Todd and Teddy took little notice of her, and she barely saw Finley except just before breakfast. They left him a portion of supper in the refrigerator each evening, and in the morning it was gone. That was the only way she knew he was eating.

Each evening at supper, LeFou would call out the dish she made, and not in a kind way. "Miss Stone prepared the onions tonight," he said with a small curl of his lip, or, "The over-cooked potatoes are Miss Stone's work." Ellie felt her ears warm, but most of the family took little notice. Except for Mr. West, who made a point to try the called-out dish and compliment it. Whether he knew Ellie waited in the servery or just knew Portia would carry the compliment to her, Ellie wasn't sure.

She passed him often during the day as she walked around the house, as it seemed he spent his days restlessly roaming. He always gave her the courtesy of a nod and asked how her apprenticeship (that was the word he used) was proceeding. Once she asked him if there was a way to get into LeFou's good graces, and he laughed. "I pay his salary," he said, "and I feel that is the only way I have managed it." She must have looked disappointed, because he said, "In your favor, my dear, at the end of the month you will not have to worry about it any longer."

She supposed that was true, and she did enjoy the company of most of the staff and family. Lavinia shared some drawings, which Ellie thought very good, and Miss Davis complimented her on Wednesday for the "professionalism" she had brought to the kitchen. By Thursday of the week, her fourth day at Fortescue, she felt comfortable as part of the household. It was hard to imagine that her time here was nearly a quarter over already.

Tea that day was cucumber sandwiches and cold tongue and cheeses, a selection of six different cheeses that LeFou picked from a basket of several and sliced himself. Ellie was sent to fetch and arrange crackers to accompany the rest, but today LeFou told her she would make the bread for tomorrow's lunch. Ellie was not terribly confident in her bread, not beside this French fox, but all the more she could learn, she reasoned.

When tea had been served, she was kept in the kitchen to begin preparations for the supper, which was to be a beef and ale stew with horseradish dumplings. William had fetched the beef with the eggs, and had left an order with the greengrocer, as they hadn't been able to fill it that morning for reasons they hadn't told him. Or at least, when LeFou asked him, he said, "they said it weren't ready," and to each subsequent inquiry repeated those words until the fox threw his paws in the air and walked away.

William, in Ellie's short experience of him, seemed the only one immune to LeFou's barks. Lorna shrank, Teddy fought back, and James might brush them off but at least acknowledged them. And for LeFou's part, he did not berate William for not completing the order but seemed most angry at the greengrocer.

Shortly after that, a badger came into the kitchen, and Ellie's first reaction was to drop what she was doing (mixing the dough for the dumplings) and say, "Oh, ma'am, what do you need?"

"No need to ma'am me. Stone, is it? Ellie, right?"

Only then did she recognize Georgette, as the badger dumped a sack onto the counter. "That's right," she said. "These will be the onions, mushrooms..."

"And carrots. It's all there."

Now LeFou took notice. "And about time, too," he snapped. "Why could these not be sent with William in the morning?"

Georgette didn't back down. "They wasn't ready in the morning," she said. "Can't send what we don't have."

"Why not? Did they arrive fresh this afternoon?" He picked one of the onions out of the sack. "Clearly not."

"You don't want them, I can take 'em back." She reached for the sack.

He pushed it away from her, along the counter. "They are better than nothing," he said. "But next time you may send them with William."

"We got a shop to open," she retorted. "Got other customers but you. And here they are, in plenty of time for supper, so what have you got to complain about?"

"I complain because as the customer, I ask for something, and here it arrives eight hours later."

"It's never eight hours." Georgette glanced at Ellie. "He came round at half-seven, and it's not even five o'clock now."

LeFou stared at her and then turned and stalked back to the counter next to the stove, where he continued to chop beef, but now every strike of the cleaver was twice as loud, making Ellie jump. Georgette grinned at her and then turned to the wildcat. As she turned, Ellie glimpsed the corner of an envelope in the pocket of the light jacket she wore over her dress. "Say, Lorna," she said, "or Ellie, you know where Devon might be?"

"Sorry," Ellie said.

Lorna shook her head quickly as LeFou said, "You've made your delivery and there is no longer a reason for you to be in my kitchen."

Georgette rolled her eyes and lifted one paw in a silent wave to Ellie, then left. But as she opened the kitchen door, Ellie caught the small figure of Portia on the other side. Georgette stopped and asked Portia the same question. "Haven't seen 'im," the otter said. "Sorry."

The badger frowned at that and then let the kitchen door swing shut, and Ellie returned her attention to the dumplings, her mind on the bread she was going to make the next day. The dumplings at this stage were a simple dough that she had to knead until it was smooth. Lorna had fetched horseradish sauce and parsley, so Ellie set about chopping the parsley while Lorna prepared the casserole dish and LeFou browned the beef in batches.

He was on the third and last batch when Devon appeared at the kitchen door. He leaned against it and said, "Anyone seen Georgette? Portia said she was looking for me."

"No," LeFou replied curtly.

"That was ages ago," Ellie said. "I expect she's back in town by now."

"No," Devon said vaguely, "she wanted to see me. Never mind, I'll find her." But he dithered there for a moment until Ellie looked at him and saw how flat his whiskers were. Then he said, "Is that the bag she brought? Maybe there's a note on it?"

LeFou did not look away from the beef whose scent filled the kitchen, so Ellie went over to the bag. "There's no note here," she said, turning back to Devon. "I think she did have an envelope with her, though."

"All right," he said. "I'll go...I'll go and find her, I suppose."

He looked rather like someone who was struggling to understand some bad news he'd been given. Ellie dearly wanted to ask Portia if he and Georgette had broken up, because she was sure Portia would know, but she didn't dare gossip while LeFou was in the kitchen, and anyway, the dumplings had to be assembled and then chilled in the refrigerator. After that, LeFou had her chop the mushrooms and carrots, which went into the pan when the beef was done.

"Right," he told her as he and Lorna filled the casserole dish with ale and seasonings. "Now this bakes for two hours and there is nothing more for us to do until then."

So he went off, likely to sit with Mister West, as he hadn't that morning, and Lorna tidied up the kitchen. Ellie tried to help her, but after perhaps half an hour, Lorna said, "I can manage, go on."

Ellie went to look for Portia, because the question of Devon and Georgette was still on her mind, but she didn't have a clear idea of what Portia's schedule was. Likely the otter stationed herself nearest where other people were talking and could be overheard, so Ellie checked all the rooms off the front hallway on the first floor, where a clock chimed six times from the parlor as she poked her nose into it. She walked down the West Corridor and turned onto the back hallway, but before she could check any of the rooms, she saw Todd at the far end of the hallway, down near the sun room and sitting rooms. When he saw her he startled, then ducked back around the corner and out of sight.

She frowned. Why would Todd need to hide from her? Her detective senses prickled, and so she forgot her station for a moment and followed them, hurrying down the hallway after him. She'd nearly reached the large glass doors that led to the gardens when Teddy burst through them in his military coat. He too looked startled to see her, but at least he didn't turn and run away. "What are you doing here?" he demanded.

"Sorry, sir," she said. "I've some free time, and I was looking for Portia. Are you...was it raining?"

For half of his coat was wet, dripping onto the marble floor, and his fur matted down where it was visible. He scowled. "Tripped over, and fell half in the bloody fountain." He gestured, scattering more water droplets, and hurried away down the hallway as fast as his cane would allow, toward where Todd had been. "Going to go and change."

"Of course." Ellie made a small curtsy and then spotted Portia coming around a corner at the other end of the hallway. "There's Portia."

She walked toward the small otter, who lifted a paw to wave. "I've just seen the strangest thing," she called, walking to meet Ellie.

But before they reached each other, a cry of "Oh God, oh God," came down the stairway that gave onto the hallway between them, followed closely by Devon, stumbling down the last few steps. His neat coat was askew, and he kept wiping his paws on it, eyes wide. "I...I..."

Ellie hurried toward him. He was breathing hard, looking at her but almost through her. Portia reached him as Ellie asked, "What is it?"

He stared, panting, and finally said, "I've killed her."

CHAPTER 6
THE GARDEN VIEW ROOM

"What?" Portia said, as though she'd misheard him.

"Killed who?" Ellie asked, her tone sharp.

"G-Georgette." Devon swallowed. "I—I can't believe it."

"Where? Up there?" Portia asked.

Devon nodded. "In—in the Garden View room," he said hoarsely.

Ellie wanted to run up and look, but she knew it was more important to get Devon's statement. "What happened?" she asked gently.

He turned his eyes to her, and she saw the shine of tears in them. "She, ah, I can't believe it, still. She said she knew I was running 'round with one of you, and I swore I wasn't, but she came at me with a knife." He showed the sleeve of his shirt, which had a long rent in it. "I picked up a poker to defend myself, an' she came at me again. I swung an' hit her an' she dropped. She didn't get up." He pressed his paws to his face.

At the top of the stairs, a black and white muzzle looked down, and James's familiar burr called, "What's happened? I heard a noise."

"Don't go in the Garden View Room!" Portia called.

James's muzzle swung behind him. "Whyever not?"

"I'll go and look," Ellie said to Portia. "You've got him?"

"Yes. Come on, Dev," Portia said, sliding a paw behind his back and guiding the larger otter down the hallway.

Ellie hurried up the stair, around the dogleg, and up to where James had just reached the top. "Let me come with you," she said.

"What's happened in there?" he asked.

Ellie hesitated. "Devon says he's killed someone."

"What?" The easygoing manner disappeared with that sharp word, and James propelled himself with his walking-stick along the upstairs hallway.

"Which one is the Garden View room?" Ellie guessed it would be on her right, on the side of the house that faced the gardens, but there were three doors and two of them were open.

James pointed with his stick. "This one here, but..." He caught her wrist. "I pray you attend me, Miss Stone. I fear it is a sight not proper for a young lady to behold. I once had the opportunity to see a murdered deer, and it was a terrible sight. I was coming home late—"

"I've seen a dead body," Ellie said. "Three of them, in fact."

The old badger's eyes widened. "In the city during the war, I presume. I am so sorry to hear it."

"No; just in the course of my service."

James uttered a short cry of surprise. "My dear, you have uncharted depths. You must share these stories with me once we have sorted this tragic matter."

Going at James's pace gave Ellie an extra few seconds to imagine what might be in the room. She couldn't help but remember finding the body of Giles St. Clair, and the feeling of nausea and horror echoed through her as she approached this door, steeling herself for what she would find.

Perhaps because she was expecting it, the sight that met her and James when they reached the door didn't distress her very much. Georgette lay on the floor, as she expected, wearing the same light blue dress and jacket she'd been wearing an hour or so earlier in the kitchen. Like poor Mr. St. Clair, however, there was no doubt she was dead. She'd fallen on her back, arms flung out as though she'd tried to steady herself, and her eyes stared glassily up at the ceiling.

She lay on a blue and green patterned carpet in the center of a room dominated by the two large windows that let out onto the garden. Both chairs in the room faced the windows, and below each window was a small side table with flowers. A similar vase of flowers lay overturned next to a small table that had likely stood between the two chairs. Georgette lay on the carpet between the chairs and the windows, so the afternoon light streamed in over her body, casting shadows behind her, and that's why it took Ellie a moment to notice that some of the dark halo around her head was blood and not shadow.

To the right of the chairs stood a small bookshelf and writing-desk, and to their left sat a fireplace. One of the pokers remained in its proper place in the stand; the other lay mostly in the fireplace, only the handle lying on the hearth. Ellie's gaze lingered on the poker, because Devon had said that's what he used, and without thinking, said, "It's summer. Why are there ashes in the fireplace? We haven't laid a fire all week."

"Callie and I sat here last night," James said, distractedly, "and we laid in a fire because the room was chilly. She really is dead, isn't she?"

"It looks that way." Ellie pointed to Georgette's head. "There's a bit of blood there."

"Oh, my dear." James tottered over to her and attempted to brace her, even though he was looking more unsteady on his feet than she was. "Really, you ought not be here right now. Let me, ah..."

His grip on her arm went from bracing to pulling, and Ellie

turned just in time to support the old badger's weight as he leaned on her. He breathed quickly for a moment or two, and Ellie held his arm firmly. His other paw came up to hold onto her and landed square on her breast, lingered there too long, and then moved, but not all the way off. "Maybe you should sit down, sir," she said, trying to twist her torso to move his paw. "Just try to breathe evenly."

"Yes," he said, finally allowing her movement to shift his paw to her shoulder. "You're right, I...I should."

"But not in here." Ellie took another look over her shoulder at Georgette. Something glinted in her right paw—the blade of a knife. "Where were you sitting?"

He pointed out the door. "The study, up here. I was writing a letter. It's just a few doors down."

It occurred to Ellie that even if she couldn't continue her investigation of the murder scene, here was likely the closest possible witness. "Did you hear any disturbance?" she asked.

"Only Devon calling, 'Oh God,'" James said. "There was some noise when they came upstairs a bit ago, but nothing other than that. I heard the door close—maybe twice, come to think of it—so I wouldn't have heard anything in that room anyway. And my hearing isn't what it once was, you know. I can't believe he really killed her. Such a terrible accident here at Fortescue. There hasn't been anything like that since..."

"Since when?" Ellie prompted when he didn't go on. They had made it halfway to the study. As they passed the staircase, she heard activity and voices below.

"There was a legend...when Callie's father bought the house, they said there'd been a murder here." James stared ahead. It was a sign of how distressed he was that he did not try to tell the entire story. "I think it was in that very room."

"I see." A murder that none of the family was involved in was not as interesting as something that had happened to people currently living here. "Here we are. Almost here. Would you like me to get you some water?"

His breathing had steadied, but there was still a little rasp to it. "Yes, my dear. That would be lovely, thank you. I feel much better now. Don't know what came over me. Of course I've seen worse than that. It must just be an illness of some sort. Do you know, something similar happened to me in Westminster one day—"

"Of course," Ellie said, guiding him to the door. "Let's just get you seated and then I'll fetch that water for you."

When she had settled James into his chair, she left the room, leaving the door open, and found Miss Davis and Mister West just reaching the top of the staircase. "What are you doing here?" the tall rabbit asked sharply.

"I was in the hallway with Portia when Devon came down, ma'am," Ellie said. "Mister MacTavish was here as well, but he's not feeling well, so I sat him down and I'm just fetching him some water."

"Go on with that," Miss Davis said, "and then get back to the kitchen and help with supper."

"Yes'm."

Ellie made for the stairs, but Mister West stopped her. "Did you go into the room with James?" he asked.

She hesitated a moment and then nodded. "Yes, sir."

"Touch anything? Move anything?"

"No, sir. Of course not."

"Did James?"

"No, sir. Well..."

He turned his black and white muzzle directly toward her. "You're hesitating."

"Well, sir, we went into the room, and I saw where she— Georgette, that is—where she was lying, and I asked why there were ashes in the fireplace, and Mister MacTavish told me there'd been a fire laid in last night, but I was looking at the fireplace, away from him, and then he sort of fell against me and I had to catch him."

"Yes?" His expression was firm, his tone gentle.

"He might have taken something off the chairs. The side table was knocked over, and he didn't reach down to the floor, but I can't swear he didn't take something off the chairs before I noticed it."

"Of all the nonsense," Miss Davis said. "Whyever would Mister MacTavish do such a thing? Go and fetch him his water, and no more of this, Miss Stone."

"Yes'm," Ellie said, and hurried down the stairs, but she felt Mister West's eyes on her until she rounded the dogleg.

She fetched the water for Mister MacTavish, who thanked her kindly, and then she returned to the kitchen, still feeling dazed. Was it possible that this had happened? Another murder? Her mind reeled, and then she reined it in. Think, she told herself. Was there anything odd about the room? Something had felt a little off, and then she'd been distracted by Mr. MacTavish and his paws.

The kitchen smelled of beef and the rich sauce of the stew. LeFou was peering into the oven, but his ears flicked as Ellie came in, swiveling toward her. "Some time yet, I think," he said, standing up. "What are you doing back here?"

Lorna, who was chopping greens, also turned to look at Ellie. The weasel composed herself breathlessly. "There's been a death," she said, and then realised that that sounded unnecessarily dramatic. "It's Georgette. Devon hit her in the head and she's died."

LeFou's ears flicked for a moment and then he grunted and looked back at the oven. "Supper is in an hour."

"I know." Ellie turned to Lorna, whose mouth was open in a small 'O'. "Miss Davis and Mister West were going to look when I left to come back here."

"Was she really dead?" Lorna asked in a whisper.

"Yes—"

"Dead or no," LeFou said, "this stew will come out of the oven in an hour. Ellie, help Lorna with the greens and then prepare your dumplings."

Chopping greens did not require a great deal of thinking, so while she helped Lorna with the large green cos leaves, she thought back over what she'd seen in the Garden View room. It all seemed perfectly straightforward to her: Georgette had a knife and had attacked Devon—she'd been insistent on seeing him, and he'd been agitated before he went up, so likely he knew she was angry—and then she'd swiped at him and he'd panicked, swung the poker, and unfortunately killed her. Georgette's head had lain toward the fireplace; Devon had probably hit her and then dropped the poker into the fireplace and staggered out.

Am I getting accustomed to murder? Ellie asked herself. Her heart still beat quickly when she thought of it, and she did wish very much that Abby were here in the house so she could get some comfort in the rabbit's arms. But she hadn't known Georgette well, and this was after all the fourth dead body she'd seen.

It was odd about Todd, though. Was that what Portia was going to tell her about before Devon interrupted them? In Ellie's police novels and in her experience, two strange things that happened at the same time were probably related. And if there were three, counting Todd's strange behavior, then two of them almost certainly were.

But she couldn't find out what Portia had been going to tell her until after dinner was served, and she couldn't ask around to find out what Todd was doing until then either. Her review of the murder scene in her head yielded no further insights, at least, not before the salad was done and she had to occupy herself with preparing the dumplings to go into the oven when the stew came out.

Miss Davis swept into the kitchen just as LeFou had taken a cube of beef to test it. "Supper will be delayed," she said. "Likely half an hour, perhaps forty minutes."

She turned to leave, but LeFou, unruffled, said, "No."

The rabbit stopped with one paw on the door. "I beg your pardon?"

"The stew will be ready in half an hour," he said. "Supper will be served then. If the family wish to eat it cold half an hour later, that is their business."

Ellie could not remember having seen anyone stand as stiffly as Miss Davis stood in that moment. "I am head of staff," she said in a voice that raised Ellie's hackles and made her take a step back. "And supper will be served at eight o'clock. Surely you can keep a stew warm for half an hour."

"If you wish the stew to be too thick and the beef to be dry, by all means," the fox said, "but I will not serve it. You may do so, but I wash my paws of it."

"The police are here to investigate the murder," Miss Davis said. "And so supper cannot be served at seven-thirty. It simply cannot happen."

"Very well." LeFou threw his paws in the air. "I leave supper to you, then." And he stalked out of the kitchen past her, bushy red tail held high as he went.

"Of all the..." Miss Davis caught herself and looked around the kitchen. "Lorna, can you manage the supper?"

"Oh," the wildcat said. "I..."

"Of course." The rabbit turned. "Miss Stone, can you manage it?"

"Yes'm," Ellie said quickly. "It's mostly done. We've just to keep it warm."

"Excellent. You have the kitchen, then." She spun around so that her dress billowed out, and disappeared through the door.

Ellie and Lorna stood for a moment and then Ellie grabbed one of the oven pads. "Let's take the stew out," she said, "and at quarter to eight, we'll put it back in with the dumplings. I can add some butter to the dumplings so they won't be dry from waiting so long, and in the meantime we can heat the stew on the hob so it keeps warm."

"That's smart," Lorna said.

Ideally, there would be some liquid Ellie could add to the stew to keep it from thickening too much, but she didn't want to add more ale, because the alcohol wouldn't have time to cook off. She settled for a little water, stirring it in gradually until the stew had evened out. "There," she said. "The greens are ready, are they?"

"Yes'm," Lorna said. "And there's some bread left over from yesterday."

Ellie's second loaf had been more successful than her first. "Excellent," she said. "Get that out and warm it up, and we'll serve a lovely supper when the family's ready."

Lorna nodded and went to fetch the bread. Ellie looked around the kitchen. "Most of the work is done," she said, "and we can take it the rest of the way." So Ellie put the murder out of her mind as best she could and prepared to serve her first supper at Fortescue Hall.

It was twenty to eight, and Ellie had just taken the dumplings out of the refrigerator and cut them into shape when William came into the kitchen, cleared his throat, and then said without preamble, "There's a constable here, he wants to see Miss Stone. Where's the paring knife?"

"Bother," Ellie said. "Lorna, can you manage the dumplings? They're cut; all you have to do is arrange them in the stew pot and then put it in. I'll set the oven."

"Oh." Lorna stared. "I'd rather you do it before you go."

"He asked for you to come right now," William said. He seemed bolder when LeFou wasn't in the kitchen, or maybe it was because he had a task to carry out.

"All right." Ellie set the oven and then stalled for a few

seconds with a question. "What did you mean about the paring knife?"

The hedgehog pointed one claw across the kitchen at the knife block. "The paring knife is missing. Cleaver is in the drying rack, utility knife is on the board there next to the greens. They were in use so it's all right they aren't put away. But the paring knife isn't anywhere."

Ellie blinked. "Georgette had a knife. Could she have taken it when she came into the kitchen?"

Both William and Lorna stared blankly at her. "She had a knife in her paw," Ellie explained. "A short one, like a paring knife."

"You saw her body?" Lorna whispered.

Ellie hesitated, then set about placing the dumplings in the pot. "I did," she said.

"Miss Davis said for you to come now," William told her.

"What did she look like?" Lorna asked, still in a hushed voice.

Ellie searched for the right words that would be honest, not too scary, and would still satisfy Lorna's breathless anticipation. "It was rather horrible," she said, placing the last dumpling. "She was just lying on the carpet staring at the ceiling."

"Miss Davis said for you to come now," William repeated.

"Yes." Ellie wiped her paws on her apron and then removed it. "I'm coming."

CHAPTER 7
THE SECOND STUDY

William hurried on his short legs through the hallways, but he knew his way better than Ellie did, and twice she felt on the verge of losing him. He led her back to the back hallway and up the stairs, and then they turned right, toward the Garden View room.

The door had been closed, and a small sign that read "POLICE ONLY" hung on the door. "Over here, miss," William said, pointing to the door opposite.

It stood ajar, and inside there was a room very similar to the one Ellie had left Mister MacTavish in just a short time ago. A brown carpet with a floral pattern lay in the center of the floor, and under a window on the other side, a wooden desk and chair sat. This room didn't have a fireplace, and around the walls hung some (to Ellie's eye) unremarkable landscapes in equally unremarkable frames.

Next to the desk, between the two windows, a small bookcase half-full of books not interesting enough for the library took up the wall space, and under the second window, a red deer in a uniform sat in an overstuffed armchair. He looked up as Ellie entered. "Miss Stone, is it? Come in, sit down." He flipped the small notebook in his fingers to a new page.

There was nowhere for her to sit except the chair at the desk, so she crossed the room and sat down there. The constable wrote something in his notebook and then looked up at her. His antlers were about half-grown, but he still looked imposing and serious. "So," he said in his Midlands accent, "James MacTavish said you were with him when he discovered the body. What—"

"Oh, he didn't discover the body," Ellie interrupted. "I'm sorry to interrupt."

"Ah." He flipped back a page, made a mark, and then flipped back. "Perhaps you could tell me in your words how it happened."

So Ellie told him about Devon coming down the stairs, about how James had come halfway down and she'd walked with him to the murder scene, how he'd felt ill and she'd walked him back to the study. "I see," he said, taking notes. "Are you prepared to swear that neither of you touched anything in the room?"

"I didn't," Ellie said. "I don't think James did."

"He swears he didn't." The deer nodded. "And you heard, er..." He checked his notes. "Devon...confess to the crime?"

Ellie nodded. The constable went on. "He said, quote, 'She came at me with a knife, I picked up a poker, swung and hit her, and she dropped.' Is that right?"

"As best I remember."

"Very good." He closed his notebook. "Thank you, miss. This seems like a very simple case. Unfortunate. I'll take young Devon to the station and we'll hold him, but I wouldn't worry too much. It's manslaughter, but in self-defense, and Mister West has already said he'll pay the costs."

"That's very generous of him," Ellie said, standing.

"Mister West is well thought-of in the village," the constable said. "My da remembers before his da bought Fortescue. Going to seed, it was, and not much to recommend the village. But having 'im here and the family has meant a great deal to all of us."

"I've been here less than a week, but it's clear he cares for this family and village." Ellie didn't quite know what else to say. "Even without having spoken much to him."

"Oh, yes." The deer lifted his head. "You're to see him after we're done here. He's in the next room down."

"He is?" Ellie looked toward the door, startled.

"Said he'd be there. I've not checked, but he seems a fellow of his word. And we're done now, so off you go."

She looked at his notebook as she turned. If it had been Sergeant Cooke, she'd have asked him to share what he'd learned, and the wolf would have gladly. But Cooke was up at Leicester now, a good half hour away, and besides, if she called him to come down, he might want to have dinner as well as looking at the case. Strike that; he definitely would want to have dinner.

And after all, Devon had confessed, and he hadn't meant to do it, so that should be an end to it.

Back in the hallway, she tried to work out which was "the next room down." In one direction was the room she'd left Mister MacTavish in, and he was likely still there, so she walked in the other direction and peered into the open doorway.

This room looked similar to the one the constable was sat in, except that the windows had been opened, and this room had no desk, but four comfortable chairs, a fireplace, and a coffee table in the middle of the chairs on which sat a vase of freshly-picked flowers. In the chair at one end of the coffee table sat Mister West, in a rumpled shirt, no tie, and slacks with suspenders. He held a pen in one paw and a small leather-bound notebook in the other, and several ink spots stained his white shirt.

He looked up over wire-rimmed glasses with a grave expression. "Miss Stone," he said. "Come in, come in. And close the door behind you."

She complied and then walked over to the chairs. He offered her any of the other three seats, and she chose the middle one, neither closest nor farthest from his chair. "Why did you want to see me, sir?"

Mister West tapped the pen on his notebook. "It seems very straightforward, doesn't it? There's a fight, the young lady pulls out a knife, Devon takes the poker and defends himself. Kills the girl by accident."

"That's what he said," Ellie said. "Very sad indeed."

The badger said, "Sad? Oh yes, of course it's very—" and then stopped and tilted his head. "What do you mean, 'that's what he said'? Do you doubt Devon?"

"Oh." Ellie's ears flushed and she folded them down. "I didn't mean anything by it. I didn't see it happen, so I can't swear as that's how it went, but it does fit. He said he killed her by accident with a poker, and there was a poker in the room, and she did have a knife in her paw. Only there are a few things that feel odd to me."

The old badger nodded. "Such as?"

"Well, the knife. I think it might be the paring knife from the kitchen, and she did linger over by the knives when she came in to ask where Devon was."

"So she came into the kitchen to ask about where he was." Mister West made a note. "That is interesting."

"She couldn't find him in the room, I suppose," Ellie said.

"She didn't mention what she wanted to see him about?"

"No." Ellie shook her head. "She was belligerent with Mister LeFou and then he ordered her out of the kitchen. She did have a note or envelope in her pocket; maybe she wanted to give him that."

Mister West gave a slight smile. "Not an uncommon occurrence, I wager. People being belligerent with LeFou, I mean."

"Well..." Ellie hesitated. "I think most of the staff are afraid of him."

The badger inclined his head slightly and fixed her with his gaze. "Are you?"

Ellie gathered herself before answering. "I think he could well do harm to my reputation, and I would not like that. But otherwise...no. I understand why he isn't well liked, but...he puts his work above all else. I would not work long in his kitchen, but I can learn a lot from him."

"You can indeed." Mister West gestured with one paw. "You said the knife felt odd to you."

"If it is the knife from the kitchen..." She trailed off until Mister West prompted her. "I mean, then...I can't work out why she took it."

"For protection? Devon may have conveyed his displeasure in a message to her asking for the meeting." He tapped his notebook. "I have reason to think he might have been angry with her."

"But then...why not bring a knife from the greengrocer's? If she knew she would need protection?"

"Oh." The old badger rubbed his muzzle. "I see. You think she may have heard or seen something upon arriving that made her feel she needed a knife."

"Yes. But I don't know what that could have been." Ellie thought back to Georgette's appearance. "And she didn't feel agitated or worried. She just wanted to see him."

"Well." Mister West brought his pen up again. "I know you've already told your story to the constable, but would you mind very much repeating it for me? Start from when Georgette came into the kitchen."

So she told him about Georgette having a row with LeFou, about Devon coming down to look for her, about seeing Portia and Todd in the hallway—and here he interrupted her. "You saw Todd? At the end of that main hallway? That would have been down by the sun room, yes?"

"Yes, sir."

"Interesting. And this was…?"

Ellie thought. "The stew went in a little before five-thirty, and then I cleaned for a bit with Lorna. I imagine it was right around six. Yes, it was, because I heard the clock in the parlor chime."

Mister West nodded. "Very interesting indeed."

"Why is that?"

"How certain are you that it was Todd?" he countered.

She blinked. "Teddy had just come in from the garden—no, wait; he came in just after that—and anyway he wears his military coat around all the time. Todd has been wearing suits for his work at the bank, and Finley isn't back from London whereas Todd has been coming back after lunch, so who else could it have been?"

He nodded. "That logic does hold."

Ellie leaned forward. "But?"

Mister West looked up with a smile and adjusted his glasses. "You're a very astute young lady. That's why I asked you here."

"Yes, sir," Ellie said, "but, begging your pardon, you haven't told me how you know that, or why you think it wasn't Todd that I saw."

His smile grew wider and he nodded. "Quite right, quite right. If you're giving me information then I should reciprocate."

"You needn't if it wouldn't be appropriate, sir. I know you must be telling me only what's proper for me to know."

"No, my dear, I'm afraid I am simply trying to gather all the information for myself before sharing any of it, but that is selfish of me. On my archaeological digs, we learned the most when all of us tackled a problem together. Very well. Here are the answers to your questions. I invited you here because James told me that when you accompanied him into the Garden View room, the first thing you asked was why there were ashes in the fireplace. I thought that showed an astute talent for observation; you looked for something that didn't make sense. And when I talked to you afterwards, you said you couldn't be sure he hadn't touched anything. You were observing even in a moment of great emotional stress.

"As for Todd, that is simpler. Todd was going to remain in London after his work today to see a school friend. He said he would take supper in London and return on the 7:38 train."

Ellie's mouth opened, but she didn't say anything. Mister West watched her and waited. Finally, she said, "Are you sure, sir?"

"As you said, I didn't see him board the train with my own eyes, but he did leave the house this morning."

"He might have told everyone he would be gone, to give himself an alibi."

"An alibi?" Mister West arched his eyebrow. "For what? You think perhaps he had something to do with Georgette's death?"

"Maybe not." Ellie hesitated.

The old badger tapped his notebook. "You saw *someone* there. I believe you. Even if Fortescue were haunted, it would be by wolves, who ancestrally owned the house. Besides, ghosts do not normally appear in the daytime." He paused. "I believe that coincidences are rare, and when unusual things happen together, they are likely connected."

"Oh! I think that too. Sir." Ellie reined in her enthusiasm.

Mister West smiled. "I do have a theory about what you saw, but I beg your indulgence while I investigate on my own."

"Of course, sir. Whatever you think I should know."

"Yes." Mister West stroked his chin, claws lightly combing through the longish fur there. "I am your employer, Miss Stone, but in this matter—and this alone—perhaps you could view me more as, shall we say, a senior partner in the investigation. A detective to your sergeant, perhaps."

Ellie's ears warmed again, but she kept them upright. "If you feel that would be appropriate, sir."

"I do." He kept her fixed in his gaze. "I will be honest, Miss Stone, and I trust your discretion. I love my family dearly, but they are not, shall we say, the kind of people one could investigate a crime with."

"Yes, sir." Her ears remained flushed as the implications of his words washed over her.

"Right, then." He took in a breath, looked down at his notebook, and looked up at her. "Well, Sergeant, in the interest of full disclosure, I should tell you one more piece of information that relates to this murder, and in fact may supply the motive. Georgette had come here perhaps a few times a month for the last three months to see Devon, but around a month ago, I heard that Teddy had been seeing her as well."

"Ohh," Ellie breathed. "So Devon found out...that's why he would be angry with her."

Mister West nodded. "I imagine he made some threat to her and that caused her to attack him with the knife. I also believe he didn't mean to harm her, although the line between love and hate can be easily crossed. The point that bothers me a little is that I'd thought Devon to be completely devoted to Teddy's service. If Teddy wanted his girl, it feels to me that Devon would have stepped aside and felt proud that his lord had chosen his girl."

Ellie couldn't help her question. "Really, sir?"

"I exaggerate, but perhaps only slightly. War creates close bonds even when lives are not in danger, and Teddy saved Devon's."

"That does make this more complicated, I suppose." Ellie rubbed her paws together. "How certain are you that Teddy was seeing her?"

"Again..." He spread his paws. "I did not witness their trysts myself, but I heard it from very reliable sources."

"Portia," Ellie guessed.

Mister West's smile widened. "You continue to demonstrate your powers of observation."

"She seems to be everywhere, especially if something is happening. Speaking of...she told me she'd seen something odd."

"When was this?"

"Right when I saw Todd."

"Indeed." He made another note in his book. "And what was it she saw?"

"Well, I don't know. Devon came down the stairs then and said...what he said, and I haven't seen Portia since."

Miss Davis came to the door then. "Sir," she called as she opened the door. "I'm looking for Ellie, because supper must be —oh, there you are. Lorna says she needs you, and supper must be served in a quarter of an hour."

"Yes'm." Ellie stood.

"She'll be down in a moment, Patricia," Mister West said. "Please close the door."

"Sir." Miss Davis retreated and closed the door behind her.

"Now." Mister West looked up at her. "Though the case itself seems straightforward, there are some elements that bother me—and you, it seems. I have my own inquiry to make, and what do you feel will be the most profitable avenue of inquiry for yourself?"

"I should talk to Portia after dinner," Ellie said. "She often stops at night to tell us what she's seen that day, so I'm sure I will see her before tomorrow."

"Excellent. For my part, I believe I can conduct my inquiries tonight as well. You will be occupied for breakfast and lunch tomorrow, but perhaps after lunch we can meet again?"

"Yes, sir." She curtsied. "Oh, and if it's possible to find out what was in the envelope Georgette had."

"Of course. Off you go, then."

She left the room and closed the door behind her. The staircase to her right beckoned, and she took a step in that direction, paw reaching out for the polished wooden banister, and then she stopped. The hallway to her left stretched quite a long way, as long as the main hallway below, she thought. She hadn't been up to this part of the house before today, and she wondered...

So she turned and walked briskly down to the end of the upstairs hallway, where it bent to follow the curve of the house. This part would lead eventually to her quarters, she imagined, but passing through a good portion of the house she hadn't seen. She'd been told to take the servants' stairs by her quarters. This hallway smelled of the boys, mostly: Todd and Teddy and Finley. Their bedrooms were along here but was there... yes. There at the corner was another stair. And when she walked down, she emerged at the far end of the main hallway, in the place where she'd seen Todd.

So, she thought, there was another way from the hallway down here to the Garden View room. The person she'd seen could easily have been on his way to or from there. She pondered that on her way back to the kitchen.

CHAPTER 8
THE DINING ROOM

Without LeFou, there was much more for Ellie to do, and she lost herself in the preparation of dishes, which had to look good, and in sorting out the stew so that it was the right consistency. She emerged from the kitchen with a dinner she was sure LeFou would not approve of, but it was the best she could manage. "Beef and ale stew with dumplings," she said to the assembled family. "Fresh greens, and fresh-baked bread." She was aware as she said it that the bread had come out of the oven hours ago and was room temperature now, but it was still baked fresh that day. She should have warmed it in the oven while they were preparing the serving dishes, but she only thought of that now.

Mister West gave her an encouraging smile as she presented the dinner. Next to him, his sister Callie sniffed and said, "The stew looks off."

"Supper is half an hour late," Mister West pointed out.

"LeFou would have found a way," she retorted.

Ellie did not explain that LeFou had abandoned the dinner specifically because he couldn't find a way, or at least couldn't be bothered, which felt very relevant. "I'm sorry, ma'am," she said.

Next to Callie, James seemed distracted, but did break in with a gruff, "Stop hectoring the girl, Callie. It's not her fault. Don't you recall..." But he trailed off rather than launch into a story.

Neither Todd nor Finley was back from London, which Ellie thought curious as she was sure she'd seen *one* of them. Teddy sat with Bonnie, both of them silent between two pairs of empty chairs. Bonnie flashed a look at Ellie as the weasel set the dishes down, but didn't say anything, and Teddy stared at his empty plate.

With Ellie taking over head chef duties, Lorna served each of the family members, ladling stew into their bowls and adding a dumpling with wooden tongs. But where there was usually chatter about how everyone's day was, now the mood was subdued, and only Callie spoke, to say, "The dumplings look good, at least," in what felt to Ellie like an attempt to make up for her previous comment.

When dinner had been served, she returned to the kitchen, passing Portia in the servery. She wanted to ask the otter about what she'd seen, but without LeFou, Ellie had to manage the supper for the staff, so there wasn't time. The remainder of the stew sat on the stove; Lorna ladled it out into bowls and set the bowls on the small table in the staff room off the other side of the kitchen. Portia would attend to the family's supper and would get her own afterwards.

The staff, too, were somber as they ate. There were not enough chairs for all of them, so there was no obviously empty chair for Devon, but his absence was notable regardless. Miss Davis set the tone the moment she walked in. "There will be no discussion of this afternoon's unpleasantness," she said.

None of the staff wanted to disobey her, but there was clearly nothing else to talk about, and so they ate in silence, with the exception of Wilkins, the old deer, who poured his stew into a wooden bowl he'd brought. "Gon' eat out in the garden," he said. "Them kids was back, digging up perfectly good path. Gon' stay up an' catch 'em at it this time." And without waiting for acknowledgment, he nodded to them and left the room.

Nobody else spoke until Miss Davis finished her dumpling and greens and set the bowl down. "You did well with supper, under the circumstances, Miss Stone," she said.

"Oh. Thank you, ma'am," Ellie said. LeFou had not come to eat with the staff; she supposed he had his own store of food, or else he'd gone down to the village.

"Let us hope it is not necessary again." The rabbit dabbed at her lips and then left without another word.

As soon as she'd left the room, hushed whispers broke out. Portia told everyone how Devon had come down the stairs, and Ellie had to tell about going upstairs with Mr. MacTavish to find the body, her protestations that Miss Davis had forbidden this conversation ignored. The junior housemaid said that she'd never trusted Devon, and Lorna said Devon was "a good fellow."

"He said he did it," Portia reminded them, "and who else could have? There was only Mister MacTavish there at the staircase, and why would he have killed poor Georgette? And why would Devon have said he did if he didn't?"

Ellie didn't think this the right time to mention that she'd seen Todd at a part of the hallway near a staircase. But Lavinia, who'd remained quiet until then, said, "He'd say he did it to protect Teddy, wouldn't he?"

"Teddy wasn't even in the house." Portia stared down at her plate, pushing the stew around with a spoon.

"No," Ellie confirmed. "He'd been out in the garden walking."

"He might protect Teddy's grandfather as well," Lavinia mused. "Families are curious like that. Teddy and his grandda got on well."

"Everyone gets on well with *Mister* MacTavish," Portia said. She lifted the spoon to her muzzle and slurped noisily.

"The paring-knife is still missing from the kitchen," William said unexpectedly.

"We think Georgette took it when she came in," Ellie told him.

"But it's still not there."

"No, the police will have kept it," she said.

The hedgehog rubbed his paws together. "When will it come back?" he asked softly.

"I don't know," Ellie told him. "We can ask the police. I don't expect they'll need it for more than...a week, perhaps? Portia, did the constable say anything about when they'd return the knife?"

"What?" The small otter looked over at Ellie. "What knife?"

"The paring-knife from the kitchen. William is anxious to know when it might be returned."

"Why?" Portia dismissed the subject. "It's been used in an attack. Why would we want it back? Excuse me, I have to go now." And she hurried out of the room.

Ellie debated whether to follow her, but Portia would come by their room in an hour, she was sure. She told William she would ask about getting a new knife to replace the old one, and that satisfied him; then Ellie went out to the kitchen and told Lorna she would manage the washing up so the wildcat could eat.

When she finally did go upstairs to her room, it was with a sense of accomplishment. She'd managed supper on her own. Granted, it was with LeFou's stew, but Ellie had finished it, had served it, and the family had appreciated her work. She wished the circumstances might have been a little different, but one couldn't help that.

Even Lavinia complimented Ellie's handling of dinner. "Stepping in at the last minute can't have been easy. That LeFou never considers how what he does makes more work for anyone else."

"I think he considers it," Ellie replied. "I just don't think he cares. But thank you."

"Anyway," Lavinia said, "what a frightful day. Poor Georgette. I thought something like this might happen to her, you know."

This turn surprised Ellie. "What? That she'd be murdered?"

"Oh, no, perhaps not that, but...she seemed to make a study in how to get into a person's fur. It never worked with me, but she would always make these little remarks, things that seemed innocent enough, but which were meant to make people feel bad. Like she would prepare carrots for William and would say, 'I've ordered them from largest to smallest, just like you like.'"

"That doesn't sound bad," Ellie said.

"But William doesn't care about the size of the carrots, or how they're ordered. He is particular about other things, so it's meant to make him feel self-conscious about that, even though she's doing a nice thing for him, putting the carrots out. Only it doesn't work on William, either. With me it's because I just don't care what she thinks—or 'thought,' I suppose I should say now—and with William it's because he isn't self-conscious at all. At least, he doesn't perceive it from other people. He is who he is."

"That's not a bad way to be." Ellie felt that Lavinia's repeated denials meant that at least some of Georgette's words had found a mark.

Lavinia nodded. "He lives a rather serene life. Lonely, though. Everyone looks down on him. Or they treat him like an encyclopædia. Do you really think Devon killed her?"

Ellie took her time answering. "I don't know yet," she said slowly. "It seems like it. But there's a lot we don't know."

"Unless we ask the constable, I'm not sure we'll ever know,"

Lavinia said. "So we might as well imagine. I don't think he did it. I think he must be covering for someone else."

"What if..." Ellie sat on her bed and curled her tail around her side. "What if Teddy killed her before he went out to the garden, and then Devon went up to cover for him? Maybe he made the cut in his sleeve himself."

Lavinia perked up. "Did he have a cut in his clothing? Teddy, I mean."

"No-o, not that I noticed."

"You were far away, though, weren't you?"

Ellie shook her head. "He walked right by me when he came in. He was annoyed he'd fallen in the fountain. So I was looking at his clothes, and I don't remember seeing any rips or cuts."

"Well." The rabbit shook her head. "That doesn't mean anything. She might not have actually cut him with the knife."

"True." Ellie stared into the cold fireplace. "So you think Teddy found out she was here to see Devon and got jealous?"

"Oh, she probably said something to make him fly into a rage," Lavinia said. "Teddy has a temper."

"Yes, but he's never killed anyone," Ellie pointed out.

Portia wandered into the room at that moment and plopped herself down on Ellie's bed. "Who hasn't? Devon? He surely has. He was in the war."

"Teddy," Lavinia said.

"He was too. Why are you talking about Teddy?"

"He might've killed Georgette, and Devon was covering for him," Ellie said. "Maybe he happened by when she was waiting for Devon. Did he know she was seeing Devon?"

Portia's whiskers twitched. "Of course he knew," she said. "There couldn't be anything serious between Teddy and Georgette anyway. They're both badgers."

"It's very progressive of him," Lavinia said. "I wouldn't have expected it."

"Anyway," Portia said, "why are you talking about Teddy? He was in the garden."

"But he might have killed Georgette before that," Ellie said, "and then Devon covered for him. That's what Lavinia thinks, anyway."

"You thought the same," Lavinia objected.

"No; he went out to the garden earlier," Portia said. "I saw him. He was there right after I saw Georgette in the kitchen."

"Was that the strange thing you saw that you were going to tell me about?" Ellie asked.

Portia looked startled for a moment. "Fancy you remembering that," she said. "No, that was something else. I saw a hen harrier out in the garden. Beautiful lovely bird."

"Another one?" Lavinia asked.

The small otter looked annoyed. "Yes, another one."

"Wilkins—that's the gardener—he saw one two weeks ago," Lavinia explained to Ellie. "He used to be a gamekeeper, so he wanted to shoot it, but Mister West doesn't hunt on the grounds, so he told Wilkins the harrier was welcome to whatever grouse it could find. But when Elva at the post heard about it, she crossed herself and said a harrier perched on a house meant death in the house."

"That's come true, hasn't it?" Ellie said. "And another today. I wonder if that means there'll be a second death."

"It's ridiculous," Portia said. "Superstition. Anyway, Elva said it had to perch on the house, and this one didn't, just on the fountain in the garden."

"Maybe someone will die in the fountain," Lavinia said.

Portia got up. "I don't want to talk about the harrier," she said. "Poor Georgette, and poor Devon. He didn't mean it, I'm sure."

Ellie put a paw on Portia's arm. "Do you know where LeFou went after he gave up on the dinner?"

"Why would I?"

"Because you know what everyone's doing."

Ellie worried the moment after she said it that Portia might think she was being called a busybody, but the otter seemed mollified by that. "I expect he went back to his room," she said. "I saw him going back in that direction. Why?"

"I didn't see him the rest of the night," Ellie said. "He didn't come to get supper with the staff. I thought he might have gone down to the village."

"He keeps food in his room," Portia said. "Bread and dried meat. Miss Davis is on at him about it because it attracts mice."

"Ah, that explains it. Thank you." Ellie beamed up.

The otter smiled back. "He's an odd one, but he's French. I suppose that accounts for it."

"Maybe." Ellie tilted her head. "I think he's just particular. He likes things a certain way, and when they aren't that way, he gets upset."

"You make him sound like William." Lavinia sniffed. "But William's sweet and LeFou is beastly."

"He's not so terrible," Portia objected. "He's no Mister MacTavish. Keeps his paws to himself. And William too."

"William wouldn't have any idea what to do." Lavinia had opened a sketch-book and was letting a pencil float dreamily over it.

"Lads are all lads," Portia said. "It's up to us ladies to know how to get what we want from them, that's all."

Ellie frowned. "Do you fancy William?"

"Heavens, no." Portia laughed. "I wasn't talking about him. Goodnight, dears. It's been quite the day, but tomorrow will be better."

When she'd left, Ellie lay back on her bed. "She seemed in rather a good mood, considering."

"She wasn't friendly with Georgette, not especially," Lavinia said.

"Was anyone here? Except Devon and Teddy?"

Lavinia didn't answer right away, but finally she said, "I don't believe so. Oh. I have seen her talking to Finley now and again."

"I don't think I've seen Finley for more than a few minutes," Ellie said. "He must work terribly hard in London."

"Something with banks, I think," Lavinia said vaguely.

"Yes, he works at a bank." Ellie stared up at the ceiling. "If it paid well, wouldn't he live in London?"

"Maybe he likes being here with the family. He's here at week-ends."

"He could keep a flat in London. Why come back here every night?"

Lavinia kept sketching. "I haven't really thought about it," she said. "Perhaps it doesn't pay all that well."

Ellie nodded. "That could be it." She rolled over, picked up a small notebook she kept by her bed, and began to write down all her notes about the day, before the details slipped away into memory.

CHAPTER 9
THE GREENGROCER'S

The next morning, Ellie prepared to make her omelette again, feeling that each morning she improved, but when she got to the kitchen, the fox snapped at her to make the toast. "Lorna can make the omelette today."

Stunned at this apparent demotion, Ellie walked to the counter and set about slicing bread. Lorna also seemed taken by surprise, her ears flat and whiskers trembling as she got a frying-pan out. As Ellie finished cutting the bread for the toast, Lorna brought the butter to her and asked under her breath, "How much butter should I use?"

"A large spoonful," Ellie told her, taking a generous scoop of it to serve with the toast. "But it won't matter much."

"I know." Lorna took the butter dish back. "But maybe he'll only yell at me a little."

The shakeup of the routine, less than a week into her stay at Fortescue, gnawed at Ellie, mostly because she imagined herself getting an unfavorable report. She knew Miss Davis was the one to make the report, but she would likely listen to whatever LeFou told her. So she rehearsed a reasonable way to ask about it while she made the toast, and then walked over to where LeFou was cooking the sausages. "Why am I not making the omelette today?" she asked the fox.

He didn't even turn to her, though his whiskers twitched. "You question my authority in my own kitchen?"

"I'm not questioning," Ellie said, keeping her voice level. "I just want to understand. How else am I meant to learn?"

"I did not agree to teach you," LeFou said.

"But you have been anyway," Ellie pointed out. "I understand you're upset with me."

"Why do you think I'm upset with you?" he countered.

"Because I served supper last night when you wouldn't."

"And what could you have done so that I would not be upset with you?"

Ellie frowned. "...Not? Served supper?"

"Voilà," the fox said. "Lesson learned."

"But we work for the family." Ellie's short tail lashed. "If they want supper, I have to serve it, or I'll be dismissed."

"We are not labourers here in the kitchen, but craftspeople. We are judged on the quality of our meals. If the family insists on being served a substandard meal, then they are saying, 'we do not care for the quality of your food.' They understand that they insist on it, but—" He turned the sausages and pressed them lightly, resulting in a loud hiss. "They will still judge the meal. They will find it wanting. And even though it is entirely their fault, they will blame you."

Ellie was not sure Georgette's murder and the subsequent investigation could be considered the family's "fault," but that wasn't the point of the argument, or lesson; she wasn't quite sure which they were having anymore. "You do enjoy a privileged relationship with Mr. West," she said carefully. "I don't think I have the same freedom."

"Better to be dismissed from a position where your work is not valued," LeFou shot back. "Find the job where your talent is valued and stay there."

As much as Ellie felt this philosophy ignored some rather basic realities of life, she couldn't come up with an argument against it. So she left LeFou to finish the sausages (he had ground and seasoned them himself, and they smelled excellent), and set the toast on the toast rack.

After breakfast, while Ellie was helping Lorna wash the dishes, Miss Davis came into the kitchen. "Mister West wishes to see Miss Stone in his study immediately."

LeFou turned to glare at the rabbit. "Miss Stone is occupied. There are dishes to clean, and onions to be prepared for the onion soup at luncheon."

Miss Davis folded her arms and straightened. "Mister West wishes to see Miss Stone in his study. Immediately."

The fox and rabbit glared at each other, and then LeFou said, "The kitchen is under my orders."

"The *house*," Miss Davis replied stiffly, "is under Mister West's."

Her eyes flicked to Ellie as she said that, and Ellie remembered that Miss Davis was the one who would write her recommendation. She put down the onion knife. "I'll just go quickly and see what he wants," she said, "and I'll come straight back."

LeFou's ears flattened and he turned away from her, but he didn't object.

* * *

The door to Mister West's study stood ajar, but still Ellie knocked lightly and waited for Mister West's rich baritone to call, "Come in," before she walked in. "Close the door behind you, dear," he said, and she obeyed.

He sat behind his desk in a crisp white shirt, bow tie, and flat cap, looking as if he were about to step out. "Have a seat," he said, and Ellie took the chair to the left of the desk. "Have you found out anything further?"

"Not especially," she said. "Portia said she saw Teddy out in the garden right after Georgette arrived, and it seems he was there until I saw him come in, right before Devon came down the stairs. He'd fallen into the fountain and was in a temper about it."

"Hum!" Mister West rubbed his chin. "I did not want to believe it of Teddy, but when his Devon was involved, one can't help but think...well, it's good to know. I would not like to have to tell his mother and grandmother."

"Yes, sir," Ellie said. "What about what you were investigating?"

"I haven't reached a conclusion yet," he said.

"What was in the envelope?"

"Ah," he said. "Thank you for reminding me. That is a curious point. The police said there was no envelope or note on Georgette's body. Nor was there one in the personal effects Devon surrendered at the jail."

"But..." Ellie stared. "I'm sure she had one. I saw the white corner in her pocket, and it was the shape of an envelope."

Mister West nodded. "I believe you. So perhaps we can figure out who else might have seen Georgette while she was here."

"It wasn't LeFou or Lorna," Ellie said. "I was in the kitchen with them the whole time. But I can ask Portia. If anyone around here knows, she would know."

Mister West gave a nod of approval. "Good. Now, I have an errand for you: I would like you to observe the 5:38 train on its arrival from London."

Ellie's ears twitched. "Sir?"

"The train from London that arrives at 5:38. I would like you to observe its arrival, and who disembarks from it."

"Are—are you expecting someone specific, sir?" she asked.

He smiled. "I am, but I would not like to influence your report back to me by telling you what I expect to see. Just keep your eyes open and I'm sure you will do excellently well."

"I wouldn't lie to you about who I saw," Ellie said, stung.

"I know, my dear. Well, rather, I should say, I hope so."

"If I know who to look for," Ellie pointed out, "then I'll know where to look. A lot of people get off the train."

"Not so many in Willow's End," Mister West said. "Twenty at most. And I think you will be able to tell whether there is a badger in that crowd."

"A badger?" Ellie sat up straight. "Someone who lives at Fortescue? But...they'll recognize me."

"Not if you stay hidden. And maybe not even then." He smiled again. "I'm sure you can work out the rest for yourself. I'd like to know, if they do arrive on that train, where they go."

"Yes, sir," Ellie said. "Er..."

He tilted his head. "Yes?"

"That's—that's right when I should be preparing supper," she said. "Ought I not be in the kitchen?"

He waved a paw. "Tell LeFou I've said you may go. That should be an end of it."

Ellie did not think it would be, but she stopped short of asking him to tell LeFou himself. "Thank you, sir. I'll do my best."

"I know that, too. You've done well so far." As she stood, he said, "I do have one further question."

"Sir?"

"Whom do you think killed Georgette?"

Ellie bit her lip. "To be honest, sir, I have no idea."

"You don't think it was Devon, then."

"I...don't."

"Why not?"

She frowned. "I don't know."

He pressed. "Something wasn't right? About his confession, about the room?"

"Something like that. I can't place it, though."

"All right." The badger leaned back and scratched claws along his desk. "Don't force it. It'll come to you. I'll see you after supper and you can tell me what you found."

She hurried back to the kitchen to resume chopping onions, which she had to do away from Lorna because it made the bobcat's eyes water. When she'd finished, she approached LeFou and asked when she'd be needed for supper.

"You are the assistant cook, are you not?" He glared down at her.

"Yes, but...Mister West has asked me to run an errand in town around half past five. I am not sure how long it will take, but I thought perhaps I could do a good deal of work before, and then come back to help..." She swallowed, wilting in the face of his stony gaze. "Help finish and plate."

He'd set his paws on his hips, and neither his muzzle nor his ears moved so much as a quarter inch for several seconds. Finally, he said, "I understand that you may find it difficult to refuse an order from the master of the house. I will speak to him about commandeering my staff. In the meantime, go and do his errand. And you may fetch more onions, as you have just chopped the last of them and I think we cannot expect a delivery today."

He didn't speak to her apart from short commands, such as "Take this," and "Put that there," for the rest of the morning. When luncheon had been served, he gave Ellie several tasks that occupied her through to about half past four, when she told him she'd finished them.

"Then you are dismissed," he said sourly, and turned his back. So Ellie, with an apologetic look at Lorna, removed her apron and left the kitchen. She made sure to find Miss Davis as she left and tell her that she was running an errand for Mister West, and the rabbit beamed with approval. That made Ellie feel a little better.

Walking out of Fortescue Hall down the drive to the gate, Ellie reviewed Mister West's instructions in her mind. They reminded her, in a good way, of the way Sergeant Cooke talked to her during investigations: patient, telling her to trust her instinct. Although Mister West was holding something back, which Sergeant Cooke never would have. She missed the wolf, she realized, and felt a wave of regret that he'd pushed romance when she would have loved nothing more than to be friends. Maybe there would be a way to navigate that in the future...

But that was the future and this was the present. If he were here, Cooke would tell her to go back over what she'd seen until she figured out the thing that didn't make sense. Had it been with Devon or with the room? Devon had looked shaken, of course. He'd come down and confessed to the crime. At this very moment, he was in Willow's End's small jail waiting to be taken to...where was the court in this county? Leicester? And he would likely be found guilty, but by reason of self-defence, and that would be the end of it.

And the room itself had looked very plain and ordinary, for a murder scene. The poker was there, askew in the fireplace; Georgette was there, dead on the carpet, blood around her head. Perhaps old Mr. MacTavish had taken something from one of the chairs, but she didn't think that was it. He'd seemed stricken, that was all, in the way that someone who'd never seen a murder might act. Yes, he'd let his paws roam, and maybe he'd exaggerated his distress for that reason, but that didn't mean he was guilty of anything more than that.

Did it matter what Todd had been doing down by the bedrooms? Or...or perhaps not-Todd, if Mister West was right. But if it wasn't Todd, then the only other person it could have been was Finley, who was also in London—

—unless he wasn't. Unless he was coming back on earlier trains for some reason. Such as the 5:38 train.

It had taken Ellie only fifteen minutes or so to walk up from the station with Miss Davis, and that was with her luggage and stopping briefly to talk to Georgette. Someone familiar with the village and the house could easily arrive on the 5:38 train and be at the house before six. And Finley wouldn't recognize her if he saw her at the station; of all the people in the house, he was the one Ellie had seen least.

So it had to be that Mister West thought Finley was coming back early on the train, and perhaps making a habit of it, if he expected him to do it today as well as yesterday. Would Devon have lied to protect Teddy's uncle? It didn't seem out of the question.

But she had an hour before that train was due to arrive, so she navigated the gate and set off to the village.

The air inside Fortescue Hall was warm as a matter of course, especially in the kitchen, but Ellie had not been out in the sun often enough to appreciate how much it warmed her fur. It was very like sitting in front of a fire in the middle of summer. Even the short walk to the village left her panting slightly.

She had an hour to spare before the train came in, so she started at the greengrocer's. It was a relief to step into the shade of the awning over the carts, where she joined a rabbit in a plain white dress and shawl and a fox whose patched blue dress showed streaks of dust and who was panting loudly over the celery.

A hedgehog with grey along his muzzle and ears poked his head out the door. "Apologies, ladies," he said, "I'll be with you as soon as I can. It's just me today." He tugged on the dirty apron he wore and then ducked back into his store before any of them had a chance to reply.

The fox had clearly heard why he had no help today, because she said, "Take your time, dear," but the rabbit said, "Typical," and kept picking up parsnips.

"Do you not know what's happened?" the fox asked.

"That Georgette's malingering again, I shouldn't doubt."

"Oh no." The fox hurried over to the parsnips. "Dead. Murdered." She drew out the word, with a little thrill in her voice. "Such a thing, in Willow's End!"

"Murdered?!" The rabbit looked shocked. "Bertha, how?"

"Well. That otter at the hall killed her."

The rabbit put a paw to her mouth. "Are they sure?"

"They say he walked into the dining room during supper, covered with blood. Can you imagine?"

Ellie thought about joining the conversation but did not feel she knew either of the ladies well enough to intrude, so she followed the hedgehog back into the store, looking for onions.

Three more ladies waited there, two at the counter and one shopping. The hedgehog had retreated behind the counter and was tallying the purchases of the dormouse who waited there patiently.

Ellie came around the side of the counter. "Miss, please wait until I'm done here," the hedgehog said. "I promise I'll be with you shortly."

"I only wondered," she said. "I'm working up at Fortescue Hall, but I have the afternoon off, and if you need help, I'd be glad to lend a paw for a little bit."

"Oh, no," he said automatically. "I couldn't."

"I don't mind," she said. "I'd like to help. I know why it's just you today."

He stopped tallying then and gave her a look. "You work at Fortescue," he said as though just now understanding that. She nodded. "Do you know your vegetables?"

"I'm an assistant cook," she told him. "I should hope so."

The dormouse leaned over. "Oh, let her help, Gerald. It's such a difficult day for you."

"All right," he said, and he exhaled. "I would greatly appreciate it. There are boxes in the back that I haven't had time to sort through, carrots and cabbages and whatnot. If you could sort out the bad ones and bring out the others..." He gestured to the displays in the store. "It would be a great help. I'm only open until five and those boxes have been sitting..."

"I'd be delighted to," Ellie said. "Just in back there?" She looked toward a closed door at the back of the store.

"Just there. Thank you so much," Gerald said.

Behind the door, three aprons hung on a hook. She put one on as she surveyed the back room. Over three long tables, six large boxes of vegetables sat, and to the right of the table, a dozen discarded boxes showed Gerald's progress today.

Various carrots and cabbages lay scattered on the table, so Ellie gathered them into piles and them emptied one of the boxes out and set it to the side to put bad ones into. She hummed to herself as she worked through the boxes, enjoying the simple work.

By the time Gerald came back to check on her, about ten minutes later, she'd sorted four of the boxes and had piles of carrots, cabbage, and leeks ready to take out to the store. He pawed through them, then took a look at the ones she'd discarded and gave a quick nod. "Good work," he said, and took one of the boxes out.

He came back minutes later for another, and then customers came in again and Ellie ended up bringing the last of the boxes out herself, arranging them in the display according to the ways the other vegetables had been set there. Gerald peered at her work from time to time but didn't correct her.

When she'd finished, she wiped her paws on the apron and hung it up again behind the door, then came out to an empty store and Gerald motioning her over to the counter. The door was closed; it must be five o'clock. "I can't thank you enough," he said. "And on your afternoon off, too! My dear, Ellie, was it? Ellie, you are truly an angel." He slid two shilling pieces across the counter to her. "And if you would like to leave Fortescue to earn less money in the village, I would be happy to have you." His eyes twinkled.

She took the shillings and smiled. "I'm not permanently at Fortescue," she said. "I'm only there while my family is abroad. They want me to learn from their cook."

"Oh, that fox," Gerald said. "I know him. Insufferable. Don't go learning that from him. Your temperament is a credit to you."

"The food is the most important thing to him," Ellie said. "More important than people, even. I don't think that way, but it's...instructive. And he knows so much about cooking."

"That whole hall is full of rum types." Gerald scratched his nose. "Meaning no disrespect, of course—Mister West and his family done a great deal for us here in Willow's End. But Georgette used to say—" He stopped, and his eyes grew misty. "Well."

"I know. I only met her a couple times, but I was so sad to hear."

He reached out and held her paw. "You were up there yesterday, ay? What happened? I only heard she'd been killed, an' that otter said she was attacking him."

"She had a knife," Ellie told him gently, holding his paw. "And Devon had a cut on his shirt. It looked like she tried to slash at him."

"She never." The hedgehog's brow came down. "Wasn't her way."

"I heard she could be mean," Ellie said cautiously.

"Oh, for certain she could. But her tongue was sharp enough. Didn't ever raise a paw to anyone. Didn't need to." He smiled and then wiped his eyes. "We got along well enough, though."

"I'm surprised she didn't scare off the customers."

Gerald nodded. "Some didn't care for her, but there were

some in the village liked a bit of a row, either to be part of or to watch. And she could wag her tongue as well as wield it."

"Ah, I see." Ellie turned that over in her head. "Has the constable been round to talk about her?"

"The constable? No, I haven't seen him. Should I?"

"I'm not sure. Er, how well do you know him?"

Gerald shook his head. "I barely see him. His wife does the shopping, but I don't really know her well either."

"Only," Ellie said, "I'm not sure he will be doing much investigating. Devon confessed and is in the jail, and I think the constable believes that's the end of it."

"Ah. I suppose that's for the best. Violent fellows ought to be locked up." He didn't seem to be thinking through the matter at all.

"But he also believes Georgette attacked Devon," Ellie reminded him.

Gerald paused. "I suppose," he said reluctantly, "that they might've had a fight."

"So she was seeing him?"

"Looks that way."

Ellie tilted her head. "You didn't know?"

"Oh, I knew she was sweet on someone up at Fortescue. Wouldn't walk down to the post to bring Mrs. Harbison her veggies, and that just down the street. But she'd go up to Fortescue at the drop of a hat." He tapped his snout. "Don't take me for a blind mole. No offense to Mrs. Harbison."

"Did she say anything yesterday? Was she in a mood?"

"She was, come to think on't." He scratched his cheek. "Had to tell her not to slam down the parsnips. And she told Mrs. Fetters her dress came from the lost and found. Mrs. Fetters' dress, not Georgette's."

"But she didn't say anything about what she was going up to Fortescue for?"

He shook his head. "She wouldn't, to me, though."

"Did she have family in town?"

"Nah, she was from Hoby. Forty-five minutes up that way. Father killed in the war, mother remarried, they didn't have no more use for Georgette, as I understand it. Her mother was well thought of in the town and so she didn't want to stick around."

"Where did she stay? I don't know the town well," Ellie explained apologetically.

"Mr. Chatcombe, the old fox—his wife was here just a bit ago—he runs a boarding-house next to the post. Georgette stayed there. I gave them some extra veg now and then and they gave her a deal on her room. We all take care of each other here."

Ellie nodded. "It's lovely here from what I've seen. And she didn't have any friends her own age in town?"

He shook his head. "Weekends she'd take the train up to Hoby. She had friends there. Oh. Maybe young Betsy Hargreave, the wolf. She came round the shop to talk to Georgette."

"Right. So she wasn't exactly happy here."

"Happy? Don't know as to that. But she had a job, she had a place to stay, she was saving money."

"Saving?" Ellie's ears perked up. "Do you know for what?"

"What do young people save for? To get married, to have a better life."

Ellie nodded. "You think she wanted to marry whoever it was up at Fortescue? Devon?"

"Didn't get that feeling from her. But I don't know as she would've told me."

"But she might've told you if she was planning to leave the job?"

He laughed ruefully. "Not sure she would, if I'm bein' honest. This mornin' when she didn't show, I thought, 'well, she's off somewhere, that's that.'" He looked down at his feet.

"Feel a little bad for thinkin' that. I reckon she would've told me."

"Who told you what happened?" Ellie asked gently.

"Mrs. Harbison. The mole." He gestured toward the front of the store. "When there's news to spread, she can walk well enough."

Ellie searched her mind for anything else she could ask. "Did she say anything before she left yesterday, do you remember?"

"Well..." He scratched his cheek. "She said she was goin' up to Fortescue, and I said as how they had some veg this morning already, an' she said they needed some more. Said she was going to take care of it."

"'Take care of it,'" Ellie echoed. "Those were the actual words?"

He nodded. "Best I can recall."

"All right," she said. "Thank you so much, Gerald. Will you be all right here tomorrow?"

He smiled warmly. "I'll call my sister's girl. She's fifteen and Mary's been wanting to find her work. But if you have an afternoon off..." He rubbed his fingers together. "There'll be a couple shillings waiting for you here."

"Thank you," Ellie said, sincerely, and went to collect the onions she'd been told to get.

CHAPTER 10
THE 5:38 FROM LONDON

She had time to walk down to the Chatcombe's boarding house next to the post, just a block from the train. Fortunately, Mrs. Chatcombe sat on the front porch peeling parsnips into a basket, still in the same dusty blue dress. It didn't look shabby, though; she felt perfectly in place among the weathered boards of the porch, in front of the clean windows with little bits of dust in the corners.

"Good afternoon," Ellie said politely.

The fox flicked her ears, stopped peeling, and squinted at Ellie even though Ellie was the one shading her eyes from the sun. "Afternoon," the fox said.

"My name's Ellie Stone. I'm up at Fortescue Hall. I wonder if you have a few minutes? Might I talk to you?"

The fox went back to peeling. "You c'n stand there an' talk. I won't stop you."

Ellie rubbed her paws together and reconsidered her approach. Mrs. Chatcombe had been so eager to tell others about the murder... "I just wanted to know a little more about Georgette. It was so terrible what happened to her."

"Aye." Mrs. Chatcombe dropped the peeled parsnip into the basket and reached for another.

"I mean, just thinking of it...I was the first one to see her body, and I hardly knew her at all."

The peeler stopped halfway down the parsnip, and the fox's grey-speckled ears perked in her direction. "You saw the body?"

"Oh, yes." Ellie feigned an appropriate amount of distress. "I'd be glad to tell you a little about it, if you like. It was rather horrible."

"Come and sit, dear." The fox patted the bench next to her. "If you've something to get off your chest, why, foxes have big ears for listening."

I'm sure you do, Ellie thought. More currency next time you're out shopping. But if it would get her some more of Georgette's background, she was happy to share the story. So she told Mrs. Chatcombe about Devon coming down and saying he'd killed her—not covered in blood, not into the dining room—and about finding the body with old Mr. MacTavish.

"So there wasn't much blood?" The fox seemed disappointed. "And her struck in the head and all?"

"Not too much," Ellie said. "Just on the rug around her head. It didn't spread too much."

"Course not. Nice thick rugs they have up there," Mrs. Chatcombe said.

"I don't suppose she told you much about why she went up to Fortescue," Ellie said.

"Oh! I've better things to do than listen to the natterings of young things about whatever's flitting through their mind at the moment," the fox said, from which Ellie gathered that she had asked and been denied an answer. "She went where she pleased, did that one. Came here when her family kicked her out up by Hoby, settled in like she'd been raised here."

"Did she make friends in the village?"

"I don't know as to friends, but she was comfortable.

Wouldn't talk much about herself, but she had sharp eyes and sharper tongue, and that'll get you far in Willow's End."

Ellie nodded. "Who did she talk to most?"

"Oh, me and the mister here over supper sometimes, and Betsy Hargreave, she runs the newspaper stand for her parents across from the train station. She's Georgette's age, about, and there aren't many girls too old for school and not yet married here."

"She must have been lonely."

The old fox laughed. "No, my dear, she weren't lonely. Went up to Hoby some weekends, and besides, she had a young fellow at Fortescue, we knew that, and sometimes he'd see her here in the village, too."

"Really? In your rooms?"

Mrs. Chatcombe's ears lay back. "Of course not. We wouldn't allow that here. But we could tell when she'd been with her young man. Her tongue was less sharp, and she wasn't so good at smoothing her dress out." The fox winked. "And sometimes she'd be coming down from Fortescue, and sometimes she'd be coming up from the train."

"Maybe she had two young fellows," Ellie said.

"Might have," Mrs. Chatcombe nodded. "Might have. But though she wouldn't tell us his name, she talked like there was only one. But maybe she was being clever about it."

"Maybe." Ellie thought about it. "Did she seem different about him this last week?"

"Now how would you know that?" Mrs. Chatcombe eyed her. "You said you hardly knew her."

"I didn't," Ellie said hurriedly. "But it seems she was angry about something to do with Devon up there, and I don't know much about her other than that she was seeing...someone."

"Between us," the fox said, leaning in, "I think she was seeing another badger."

"Oh." Ellie pressed her paws into her skirt. "Why's that?"

"Us ladies know the things we have to do when there might be a baby, you understand? Different if the fellow isn't a fox, or a weasel. Anyway," she said, "I clean the rooms. I see some things."

"I see," Ellie said. So she had been seeing Teddy, and for a while, too. Had she ever been seeing Devon, or was that all just a ruse? It was possible that Devon had become furious at Georgette for breaking up with Teddy, defending the honor of his master. "So she wasn't happy about her fellow this past week?"

"Just two days, really. When she set her mind to something, she did it." Mrs. Chatcombe picked up the last parsnip. "Wednesday it was, she came to supper and was in a mood. Picked at the veg, said the meat was overcooked when it was not, and when I told her to mind her tongue, she said, 'Everyone says that to me and I'm tired of it.' And then she said that there'd be at least one person less to tell her that soon enough."

"Sounds like she was thinking of ending it with her badger, then."

"That's what me and the mister thought. Then when she didn't come home yesterday we figured she'd, you know, patched things up." Her paw hesitated over the parsnip. "If only. Poor girl."

"Indeed." Ellie sat there while Mrs. Chatcombe finished the last parsnip just as the clock tower tolled quarter past five.

"Well, I'm done my peeling, and you've got things to do as well, no doubt." She picked up the basket of parsnips. "I'm pleased you stopped by. I'll see you around the village, shall I?"

"I'll say hello whenever I come down," Ellie promised.

"See that you do." The fox turned, tail swishing, and went into her house.

* * *

Behind the newspaper stand, a young wolf in a pink dress with a matching hat between her ears leafed through a magazine. "What can I get for you, love?" she asked in a low voice without looking up as Ellie approached.

"Actually, I was just hoping to chat for a bit. If you're not too busy."

The wolf looked up, and Ellie saw that her eyes were red. She sniffed and brought up a kerchief to dab at her nose. "I don't know as I'd be good to chat with today."

"Oh, you've been crying," Ellie said before she could help herself. "I'm so sorry. What's happened?"

"It's just—my best friend got killed. You probably heard about it." She sniffed again. "Don't get many killings in Willow's End."

"I did hear about it," Ellie said. "It was awful. I work up at Fortescue, you see."

"You do?" The wolf peered at her. "So you must have known yesterday."

Ellie nodded. "The constable came around. But we didn't know if we were supposed to tell anyone. Word will get out, though."

"I know, I know." The wolf sniffed again. "My name's Betsy. I'm sorry. I had a good cry this morning, but I'm not done, seems like."

"Of course you're not. She was your best friend." Ellie hesitated. "May I...?"

She made to come around the counter, and the wolf looked up, hesitant, so Ellie put her arms out, and then Betsy nodded. Ellie only came up to the girl's shoulder, but she gave her a warm hug and Betsy hugged her back fiercely. "Thank you," she whispered.

"I'm Ellie," Ellie said. "You have anyone else to talk to about her?"

Betsy rested her muzzle on Ellie's head, then seemed to

realize that was too familiar, and lifted it again. "My parents, I suppose. But they didn't much like Georgie."

She released Ellie, and, mindful of decorum, Ellie retreated to the end of the stand. "Why not?"

"They said she was a bad influence on me. Ha." Betsy managed a smile. "She was sweet. But she could be sharp, and that's what people saw. She got me to stop seeing Chester."

"Chester?" Ellie asked.

"A fellow I was seeing over in Groveby." That was one town over, not too far. "It wasn't going to lead to anything and we knew it, because he's a stoat. No offence, dear—Ellie—but we couldn't have a family, and he's Catholic, you see, so he doesn't hold with surrogates. And Georgie, she told me that if he wasn't going to give me a family, I shouldn't waste more time with him since that's what I want. And now I'm going to meet this wolf down in Leicester next week, only she—she won't be around for me to tell after."

"Oh, dear," Ellie said. "Well, Betsy, I'm at Fortescue Hall all this month on a temporary job, and I'll come down here to see you, and you can tell me all about it."

"Really?" Betsy smiled at her. "That's very kind of you, but you needn't if it would be a bother."

"No bother," Ellie said firmly. "I'm delighted to get to know you. I wish I'd gotten to know Georgette better."

"I'd be glad to tell you about her." Betsy sniffed again, and the kerchief was again deployed along her long muzzle.

"As a matter of fact..." Ellie paused. The wolf tilted her head politely. "This is rather delicate, but I did talk to her a little. I understood she was seeing someone at Fortescue—which makes sense, since she was a badger—but they didn't always have their, er, meetings up at the Hall. I was only interested because..." She folded her ears back. "I hope to have a visitor here next week, and I don't want to entertain them at the Hall. I was going to ask Georgette if there's a discreet place in town."

Betsy's eyes widened. "She would tell you the same thing I will. There's the storehouse—you see it there, the big thing down the end of the street?" Ellie did see it, an old stone barn with a new-looking corrugated iron roof. "Storehouse is shared by the shopkeeps here for their goods what come up from London or go down to London. But the stock trains only run Tuesday and Thursday. So Monday, Wednesday, Friday, you can slip in the back and there's a little room. It's very cosy." She splayed her ears with a bashful smile. "There's Neutra-Scent and everything. We young folk all sort of look after it so nobody spoils it."

"I won't tell, I promise," Ellie said. "Thank you. How do I know if it's in use?"

"Oh! You'll hear when you go inside. But it isn't used all that often. I only went there once with Chester, and Georgie didn't go but once a week."

"Thank you," Ellie said. "That's very helpful. Do you know who it was Georgette was seeing up at Fortescue?"

Betsy looked back and forth. "I shouldn't say," she whispered.

"If I guess, will you tell me if I'm right?" Ellie asked, and Betsy nodded. "Was it Teddy MacTavish?"

The wolf's long muzzle nodded up and down vigorously. "That's what she told me."

"Not Devon the otter?"

"Oh!" Betsy's paw went to her muzzle. "No. She did tell me once when I asked how the people at the Hall thought about her and Mister MacTavish, she said his otter servant covered, said she was there to see him." She thought. "Maybe she was really seeing the otter. But why would Georgie lie to me?"

Why indeed, Ellie wondered. She couldn't think of a reason, but she couldn't dismiss it. "I don't imagine she did, Betsy. It's been so nice talking to you, but I have to meet someone at the train now."

"Of course, Ellie. Come back anytime. I'm here most days."

"I'd like that. Maybe we could have tea sometime."

Betsy beamed and her tail wagged as Ellie left the stand. She felt good about having learned a little more information about Georgette, but also about having been able to give Betsy some comfort and maybe a friend, at least for the next few weeks.

There wasn't much to the station, a small wooden building next to the tracks with "WILLOW'S END" on a neat white sign that faced the train. Extending out from the side of the building, the station-master's office, was a roof that covered the train platforms. Some small wooden tables, painted red, stood under the shelter of the roof, against the office wall. Ellie cursed herself for not buying one of the newspapers or magazines that she could hide behind while watching the passengers disembark.

It's all right, she told herself. Mister West said I probably won't be recognized. Probably.

So she selected the table farthest back from the tracks and sat facing the train. Nobody else was waiting in the station; few people wanted to leave Willow's End in the evening to go farther away from London. The large clock over the tracks clicked along, minute by minute, and at 5:37 she heard the train approaching. A minute later it pulled into the station.

Ellie got up just as if she were waiting for the train, standing at the head and watching the passengers disembark. There were ten, and only one of them was a badger. He wore a navy-blue suit and a neatly-tied peach ascot, and he carried a leather briefcase in one paw. This was Finley, certainly; he was too old to be Todd or Teddy, although Ellie could only tell this from the grizzled fur on his cheek ruffs. He did not even look in her direction as he stepped down from the train and walked briskly across the platform.

When the passengers had all left the station, Ellie stepped

back from the train and the puzzled view of the wildcat conductor and waved him on. She hurried to the side of the office and peered around it.

The passengers had mostly dispersed around the main street, but she caught sight of Finley walking to the newspaper stand. He stopped there, bought a paper, and then walked on across to the small public-house, where he disappeared inside.

How odd. It was possible that he returned to Willow's End but disliked his family enough that he wanted to sit quietly in the public-house with a newspaper, but in that case, why not remain in London, where there were surely more public-houses to choose from and less chance that a local would see him and report that he was there?

Maybe it was a comfort thing. She waited, leaning against the station office, and then strolled over to the public-house herself.

CHAPTER 11
THE SOMERLEYTON PINT

The public-house looked to date from the 1700s, worn stones held together with little but moss supporting a wooden roof that had last been painted before the war, and maybe not the most recent one. The sign out front had been freshly repainted, though, and read in fancy golden script, "The Somerleyton Pint."

Ellie caught the smells of ale and roast fowl, as well as the scents of a number of different people, but not many sounds made it past the door save for the low murmur of conversation. She took a breath and walked in.

The main room greeted her with stronger smells and louder murmurs. Perhaps a dozen people sat at the various tables around the floor, while behind the bar a black rat polished mugs with a dishcloth. Around the room hung banners, coats of arms that Ellie supposed were of local families, and some of them looked old enough to have been hung with the original building. The most recent, showing a badger over a shield that included crossed swords and a book, Ellie thought was probably Mister West's family crest.

However, that was the only badger in evidence anywhere in

the room. Ellie looked around long enough that the bartender's eyes landed on her and he said, "Help you, miss?"

"Oh, yes," she said, hurrying to the counter. "Only I'm up at Fortescue Hall for the month and they sent me here for Mister Finley, I mean, to bring a message to him, they said he'd be here but I don't see him."

"Right," he said, nodding. "Mister Finley often stops in for a pint here after his train gets in, the 7:38 it usually is. Leave me the message and I'll see he gets it."

Ellie blinked. The rat must have been behind the bar when Finley came in; it couldn't have been more than a minute or two. "Is there another bartender?" she asked.

"What," he asked with an amused smile, "don't trust me to deliver the message? It's only me here, but I promise I'm a trust-worthy sort. Name's Cross. Ask around if you like."

"I'm Ellie," she said. "Ellie Stone. No, I only meant—well, all right. The message is simply that," she thought quickly, "he's to come round the side door tonight please on account of the workers need the main door to be undisturbed overnight."

"Side door," the rat said. "Aye, I'll let him know."

After that, there didn't seem to be much reason at all for Ellie to stay in the pub, so she left. Once out in the street, she looked up to the second story of the building. The windows were all dark, but it was possible Finley had walked up to one of the rooms there.

To be thorough, she walked all the way around the Somerleyton Pint, and at the back of it she noticed a plain wooden door leading out to the back, to a rough dirt road that had been traveled by trucks recently. And...Ellie looked up and down the rough dirt road and then walked two buildings down. This was the warehouse Betsy had talked about, and Ellie had just walked from the back of The Somerleyton Pint to the back door of the warehouse, unseen, she was sure, by anyone on the main street.

The back of the warehouse, old stone that about matched the Somerleyton Pint, rose the same two stories as the public-house. There the similarity ended, though; where the pub was old but well-maintained, the warehouse had clearly been neglected for a while. The back door, unpainted wood, was rotted at the corners.

Ellie listened at the door, but she couldn't hear any sounds from within. But that didn't mean anything. She tugged at the door to see if it would open easily, but it didn't, and she didn't want to risk disturbing whoever might be there. And then she heard voices inside. One was low, but the other was high and fast, and as soon as she spoke, Ellie recognized Portia. "I've never been. I can't wait!"

She withdrew from the door instinctively and then remembered she was supposed to be gathering information. But the moment she leaned back, Portia said, "Cheerio," and the voice was louder, so Ellie hurried back from the door and made as if she were walking along the path.

The door creaked open, loudly enough that she felt justified in turning around, and there was Portia, in a frilly white dress with a matching hat held between her ears, holding a bright red clutch in both paws. She met Ellie's eyes and then slipped the clutch under one arm. "Fancy seeing you here!" she said brightly. "What are you doing in town?"

"It's my afternoon off," Ellie said. "I was just walking around and found this road."

Portia accepted that. "It's the trade road, comes around to the station there for the freight, but also goes out to the London road. Lorries come through a few times a week. If you follow it half a mile that way, there's a lovely meadow. But you probably haven't time for that. Supper in a little while, isn't it? I'm heading back for it myself."

"I think we've time for a drink first, don't you?" Ellie hoped she might get Portia to tell her whether she'd been with Finley.

She gestured to the back door of the public-house. "Do they have tea?"

Portia didn't hesitate. "I always get gin," she said with a mischievous smile.

So they walked around to the front and found a small table in one corner of the house. The black rat, Cross, came over to them. "Always a treat to see you back in here, Portia darling," he said. "Gin?"

"And one for my friend. I'm buying," Portia said.

"Isn't that sweet of you," Cross said. "Back in a tick, ladies."

"Have you been in here before?" Portia asked, and before Ellie could reply, the otter went on. "It's been here since King George the Second. Or Third. One of those Georges. Two hundred years, at any rate. That coat of arms there..." She pointed to one of the oldest-looking banners, faded blue with gold thread clinging gamely to its patterns, a wolf rampant with a shield bearing three horizontal stripes. "That's the family that owned the hall back then, and until Mister West bought it."

"What happened to them?" Ellie asked.

"Don't know. Took the money and moved to Leicester or London, perhaps."

Cross returned with two gin and tonics and set them on the table. "You ladies don't hesitate to ask me if you need anything else," he said.

"Thanks, love," Portia said with a flirty whiskered smile as she reached for her glass.

"So," Ellie began as Portia sipped, "what's in that old house you were in? If you don't mind me asking."

"Oh, not at all." Portia put her glass down. "That's a warehouse where some of the businesses in town store things. I wanted some cloth for a sewing project, and Culliver didn't have it in the store, so he walked down with me to the warehouse to see if he had it here. He didn't, but he thinks it'll come in next week."

The gin stung in a lovely aromatic way, and the tonic fizzed on her tongue. "Oh, I see," Ellie said. "Making a new dress?"

Portia laughed. "Oh, no. I'm going to buy a new dress. No, the sewing project is for...I'm going to put up new drapes in my room. The old ones have been there forever, and I like something bright to look at. It'll cheer the room up a good deal."

"It should at that," Ellie said. "If I were staying longer, I would ask Lavinia to change our curtains too. They might date from one of those King Georges, as grey and old as they seem."

"Ha ha!" Portia took another drink, closing her eyes briefly. "I'd buy some fabric for Lavinia if I thought she would do anything with it besides drop it in a pile and then sketch that pile over and over again."

"I like her drawings. Everyone seems to think she's scattered, but she knows what's going on around her."

"Ha." Portia shook her head. "Lavinia has her head in the clouds. You're new, so she takes an interest in you, but she'll grow bored soon enough and then go back to her painting."

Ellie scratched her chin. "Maybe we can find a way to interest her in her work. Her mother is rather keen that she learn the duties of the house."

"Oh, Miss Davis." Portia dismissed her with a wave of her webbed paw. "The house is all she knows, and she expects it's all Lavinia should want to know as well. There's more to the world. Lavinia would be best served getting out and going to an art studio somewhere. She'll never be running a house." She leaned in. "Normally, you know, she doesn't have much truck with ladies' magazines, but I found one in her trash and an article had been torn out of it."

Ellie's eyes widened. "Which article? Oh, I suppose if it was torn out..."

Portia looked very pleased with herself. "You'd think you wouldn't be able to see it, but I had a look at the contents page, you see. It was..." She paused for effect. "A review of London art schools."

This revelation took Ellie aback only for a moment. "I think you're right," she said. "She'd be well suited to that. But how to get her mother to see it?"

"Ha." Portia was already more than halfway done with her drink. "Put it on her list of house chores and maybe she'll look at it then. She loves to stick her nose into anything around the house but ask Cross if he's ever seen her in the Sommy."

Ellie smiled, raising her glass to let the sharp, cold fizz wash over her tongue again. She didn't drink often, and already she felt warmth spreading from her stomach outward. "Do most of the staff come here on days off?"

"Course." Portia waved around. "Where else you gonna go in Willow's End? The family, they can take the train to London, but do you have an hour and a half there and back? Waste half your day on the train?" Ellie shook her head. "Me neither. But I tell you what, I'm going to London next day off. Get a nice dress or two. Maybe find myself a young fellow to go to dinner with." She giggled and finished the rest of her drink.

"You're not seeing anyone here at the village?"

"Heavens no. I mean..." Portia lowered her voice, though maybe not as much as she thought she was, and leaned in. "The boys here are all right for a night or two. Freddie over there maybe more. But they're not 'go out to London' material. I've got my sights set higher."

Ellie looked where Portia had nodded when she said, "Freddie," and saw a pair of polecats sitting at a table with ales, chatting amiably. It was impossible to tell which one she'd meant. "Do you know anyone in London?"

"Not yet," Portia said. "But I aim to."

"How did you come to be in Willow's End?"

Portia called for another drink, and Ellie refused her offer to get a second one as well. "Mum and Dad came over after the first war with a dozen others from our town, and they all settled just north of London. It was fine when I was growing up, but there were too many of us otters there. Mum and Dad only had otter friends, and I was only supposed to have otter friends. But we went to a public school, and I made so many other friends there, and so when I was eighteen, I ran away to stay with a friend." She accompanied "friend" with a smile that left little doubt about the nature of their "friendship." "But that didn't last, so I answered adverts for positions and finally got one here."

"Lucky," Ellie said.

"Oh, I don't know about that. It's not exactly the high life here. It's all right if you're Miss Davis or LeFou and your whole life is inside the house, or if you're Lavinia and you live in your own head half the time anyway, but for young ladies like us, it's stifling. Where's your regular family live, anyway?"

"Near Cambridge," Ellie said, "only it's just my mum, now. I send her money every now and then."

"Y'ever go back?"

Ellie shook her head, and could have left it at that, but the gin warmed her and she felt close to Portia. "She, ah, she wanted me to settle down with a nice fellow, and she had one picked out for me, but..."

"Not to your tastes?" Cross came over with the refill, and Portia smiled with a quick "Cheers" before returning her attention to Ellie. "I'll drink to that."

She clinked her glass to Ellie's, and both of them sipped. "Tastes are strange," Ellie said, feeling she ought to see what else Portia might know about the case. "Imagine Georgette and Devon. Wouldn't you think she'd be more likely to see one of the family in the hall?"

"You can never tell," Portia said, and then, without bothering to lean in, "but if you ask me, she *was* seeing one of the family."

"Oh, really?"

The otter nodded. "You didn't hear it from me, but one of them was on the telephone last night as I was passing by cleaning the hallway. I heard him say, 'I can't do this without her!'"

Ellie curled her fingers around her glass. "Was it Teddy?" she guessed.

Portia smiled and shook her head. She took another sip of her gin and seemed to enjoy Ellie's bewilderment for a good several seconds before answering. "It was Todd!"

"Todd?" This did not fit with anything Ellie knew. "Are you sure?"

"Of course I'm sure."

"What else did he say?"

Now Portia looked a little annoyed, her muzzle scrunching up. "He was talking about his new job, I think, but I didn't stay long enough to hear. I wasn't *eavesdropping*, Ellie. I just happened to hear it."

"I didn't mean to imply anything," Ellie hastened to reassure her. "It's interesting, is all." She decided to confide in Portia, at least a little. "I happened to talk to Georgette's friend, and she told me that she thought Georgette was seeing a badger up at Fortescue, not Devon."

"Oh!" Portia clapped her paws together, good humor restored. "I suppose it might have been Todd, mightn't it? Imagine what Callie would have said! My goodness! And she was seeing Devon at the same time, just imagine."

She seemed so excited about it—perhaps it was the effect of the gin—that she'd ignored what Ellie said about Georgette not dating Devon. "But we can't tell anyone about it. Especially now."

"No, of course not." Portia shook her head. "Poor Todd!"

It was not too long after that—Portia hadn't finished her second drink, but Ellie had finished her first and was debating whether she felt adventurous enough for another, not to mention imposing on her new friend's generosity (though a second drink had already been offered)—that Ellie looked up and saw Finley at the corner of the bar.

He hadn't come through the front, that was certain; their table was close to that door, and they noticed every time it opened. Had he come through the back, or come down a set of stairs that Ellie couldn't see from here?

Portia had her back to him, so Ellie said, "That's Finley behind you, I think."

"What?" Portia spun around in her chair and stared before Ellie could stop her. And the motion caught Finley's attention.

He stared at them for a moment and then picked up his drink and walked over to the table. He stood there looking down at them. "Portia," he said in a light baritone, and then turned to Ellie. "And you are...?"

"Ellie Stone, sir," Ellie said promptly. "I'm working in the kitchen at Fortescue."

"At..." He peered more closely at her. "At Fortescue Hall? This Fortescue Hall? Where my family lives?"

"Yes." Ellie's ears warmed. "I've given you toast twice on your way out."

"So you're working with LeFou." Finley snorted and turned to Portia. "You brought her *here* on your day off?"

"I can go where I like, and so can she. And," she turned to Ellie, "it's your day off, you don't have to call him 'sir' when we're out like this."

"Well," Finley said, "I just came in for a pint before I walk up to the Hall. Thirsty after that train ride."

The train had come in over an hour ago, and the next one wouldn't be for half an hour. But Ellie just nodded and said, "I imagine we'll be walking back soon ourselves."

"When we like," Portia added.

"Enjoy the walk when you do." Finley tilted back his mug,

gulped down the rest of his ale, and then walked stiffly out the front door.

"Well," Portia said when the door had closed behind the badger. "What do you suppose that was all about?"

"I thought you might know," Ellie said. "He's been here an hour or more."

The otter shook her head. "Not me." She looked up as Cross approached their table. "Oh, I don't think I'll have another, thank you."

The black rat came to the side of their table and looked down. "Folk come here for a bit of peace and quiet away from the world," he said, "and it's nobody's business who's here, or why. If someone was to go talking about people they've seen here, those people might find themselves unwelcome here in the future." He nodded his head curtly. "Hope I've made myself clear."

"Yes," Ellie said.

"Quite," Portia agreed. She fished in her red clutch and took out a pound note. "I expect this will cover our drinks. You can keep the rest."

Ellie's eyes were about as wide as Cross's—that was three times what she thought their drinks would have cost. What's more, she'd spotted a thick stack of notes in Portia's bag before she closed it. "Very generous, ma'am," Cross said, taking the pound note with delicate fingers. It disappeared into a pocket. "I'm sure there won't be any trouble."

"There won't be." Portia smiled at Ellie as Cross walked back to the bar. "Are you done, or shall we give Finley a bit more of a start before we walk back? We can still make supper if we wait a moment."

CHAPTER 12
THE SMALLER SERVANTS' QUARTERS

My Dear Abby,

You're not going to believe this. I haven't even been here a week and there's been a murder. I'm not sure it's a mystery yet, but there's definitely something strange about it. Devon, the valet, came down the stairs saying he'd killed someone, and I went upstairs and found the body of Georgette, a badger who worked at the greengrocer. He says he killed her, and she's dead, and the constable is satisfied, but... something about it doesn't feel right.

Mister West, the head of the family, agrees. Or maybe he's taking this chance to find out more of his family's secrets. In either case, he asked me to do a little detecting, and you know I can't resist that. So I got the afternoon off to go around town. I talked to the greengrocer and to the old fox whose rooms Georgette was letting, then a very nice wolf at the magazine stand, and you remember Portia, well, I ran into her at the warehouse. But I don't know that I discovered all that much, if I'm being honest.

From all the people I talked to, it sounded like Georgette was seeing someone up here at Fortescue, but nobody can agree on whom. They do agree that she was through with whatever relationship she had there, and it seems likely that that's what made someone mad enough to kill her. But as all my police novels say, you can't assume a motive just because it's the only one you can see. But Abby, I can't see any other motive. Georgette did tell me she could get things for people at the house here, and that's the only other thing I know about her. That doesn't help, though. Why would someone she was getting things for kill her? Unless she'd gotten something for them that they didn't want anyone else to know about, ever...oh, bother, now I do sound like one of my police novels, and not a good one.

I want to solve this case for Georgette's sake. She seems like a good person, if sharp-tongued, and if Devon is lying to protect someone, I would like for justice to be done. But I don't know if I can solve this one. Mister West thinks I can, but he's only just met me, and I suspect he may be cleverer than I am. It won't be the end of the world if we don't solve it, I suppose, but I will feel like I'm letting down Georgette and Mister West both.

Part of me very much wants to call Sergeant Cooke. Having a murder to investigate is the perfect reason to see him again without leading him on as to any possibility of another relationship. I know what you've said, but I still feel as though I'd be deceiving him if I couldn't tell him about you, and how could I do that without driving him away?

I wish you were here, Abby. You'd settle me down and you'd say something that pointed me in the right direction. I miss you, old soul.

Love,
Ellie

* * *

She looked up from the letter to the other bed where Lavinia was sketching on her pad. Despite being a rabbit, she was definitely not Abby. Still... "What do you think about Georgette's death?" Ellie asked.

Lavinia paused and then continued sketching without

looking up. "We've gone over this already, haven't we? What's the point in talking about it more?"

"Because...because we don't know the truth."

"We're not going to learn it," Lavinia said. "Probably not ever, and certainly not by talking about it."

Ellie glimpsed, then, something of what frustrated Miss Davis about her daughter. "So you're not curious at all about it?"

"I was, yesterday." She paused to study her sketch, dabbed at the pencil with a rubber, then resumed sketching. "But Devon's been arrested for it, hasn't he? The police haven't been around asking questions."

"Mister West thinks there's something odd about it, and so do I," Ellie said.

"I suppose you can tell me about it if you like."

Lavinia sounded bored, and Ellie didn't want to read aloud what she'd just written to Abby. So she asked instead, "What are you sketching?"

"Flowers from the garden," the rabbit said.

There were no flowers anywhere in the room. "From memory?"

Lavinia nodded. "I've sketched them four or five times already, so I'm interested to sketch them from memory now, to see what about them was strongest in my mind. The sketch is then my impression of the flowers rather than just representing them."

"You sketch the same things over and over?" Ellie asked. "Is that for practice?"

"A little for practice," Lavinia said, "and a little to see how each sketch is different. Sometimes I'll sketch the same thing a different way. I find a line I like, or a curve that came out well, and I try to remember how to do that again next time. Sometimes the differences reveal things to me."

Ellie took a breath. "Can't you do that same thing with...

with the rooms? They have to look a certain way, don't they? Couldn't you clean them and maybe do it a little differently each time, to see what the differences reveal?"

Now Lavinia did look up from her sketch pad. "My mother told you to get me interested in the house work, didn't she?"

"She, ah, she mentioned it, yes." Ellie's ears warmed.

"Don't worry about it. She 'mentions' it to everyone who shares this room with me. You're very considerate. You held out several days before asking." The rabbit smiled and returned her attention to her sketch. "As it happens, I suppose I can make an effort to be a little more diligent while you're here. And then when you've gone, it won't matter what I do."

"Well—thank you," Ellie said, not wanting to press on the odd phrasing there.

"As for the murder..." Lavinia's tongue poked out of the corner of her mouth as she guided the pencil along what seemed to be a difficult and convoluted path. "Oh, bother." She brought the rubber to the paper again and erased in small, quick movements. Ellie waited patiently until the rabbit had picked up her pencil and resumed her train of thought. "I suppose I understand if it's like painting for you. You feel drawn to it, to look at it over and over and make sense of it. Like your police novels."

That seemed to be all she had to say. Ellie waited a short time and then said, "But I shouldn't?"

Lavinia looked up. "Oh, I didn't mean that. Of course you should. As long as it doesn't harm anyone."

"Georgette's already been harmed. I don't think Devon did it."

"If you can't prove it, then all you have is words, and that's what I mean. Words can make people feel awful and scared." She paused. "Where is Portia? She's usually here by now."

"We came back from the town together," Ellie said. "I got our supper from the kitchen and William was still fretting about that paring knife, so Portia told him she'd buy a replacement, and your mother was there and told her it wasn't her responsibility to do that, and it seemed like that might become a bit of a row, so I came up here."

Lavinia frowned, her pencil sliding back and forth quickly as she shaded something. "Why would Portia buy a knife?"

"She likes William, and he was rather distressed," Ellie said. "And she has money."

"No, she hasn't," Lavinia scoffed. "She's always talking about wanting to save up to go to London and then she goes and buys a handbag or gets her fur done or goes down to the Sommy."

"She has," Ellie insisted. "I saw it. She gave the bartender at the pub a pound."

"A pound?" Lavinia's paw lifted the pencil from the page and her eyes widened. "Good for her, I suppose. Wonder how that happened."

Ellie was quiet for a moment. "You don't suppose it's to do with Georgette, do you?"

Lavinia gave a short laugh. "You do read too many of those police novels."

"It's another strange thing that's happened," Ellie said. "And Portia said she saw something odd right before Devon came down the stairs, but afterwards she said it was just the hen harrier."

"A hen harrier is strange, and she would know what it was. The gardener called us out to look at it. It stayed on the house for a good while, preening and looking around."

"But this one didn't stay around."

"I don't suppose they all behave exactly the same."

Though Lavinia was very moderate in her disposition, she sounded a little peeved now, so Ellie switched tacks slightly. "Did you happen to sketch the harrier? I'd very much like to see it."

"As a matter of fact, I did." Lavinia flipped back through her pad. "Oh, it's in the last one." She reached under her bed and brought out another pad, flipped through it, and then held it up for Ellie.

Lavinia had talent, that was certain. The picture of the bird evoked it very well, and Ellie got a further impression of wildness and barely contained energy, as though it might leap off the page in the next moment. "It's lovely," she said. "I can see why it would be remarkable."

But Lavinia's disinterest notwithstanding, Ellie felt there was a good deal more going on than met her eye, or at least a little more. She thought it very likely that Portia had seen something connected to Georgette's death and was now blackmailing someone to keep quiet what she'd seen. Which meant that maybe, just maybe, Ellie could corner her and get some information out of her.

CHAPTER 13
THE STUDY

But when Portia did finally come up, she only stopped long enough to say goodnight to Ellie and Lavinia before going on through to her own room. Ellie lay in bed and thought about the murder until she fell asleep.

The next morning, when Portia came through their room, Ellie was waiting. "Can I ask you something?"

"Ask me at breakfast," Portia said. "I've got so many clothes to lay out, and I've got to do Teddy's as well since Devon's gone."

"Right," Ellie said. "I'll have your buttered eggs at seven, then?"

"Perfect." Portia put a paw on her shoulder. "Yours are better than LeFou's, you know, though I'd never tell him so."

"Thank you." Warmth bloomed in Ellie's chest, although her cooking had been the farthest thing from her mind in the last day.

She met Lorna in the kitchen, and together they prepared the staff breakfast, buttered eggs with cheese and toast. Breakfast was not a social meal like supper; the staff hurried in as they had time, sat and ate, maybe exchanged a few words, then went back to their duties.

Wilkins, the old deer, stayed longer than most. "Been up

two hour already," he said, taking two pieces of toast and a plate of eggs. He peered at the eggs and then reached for the pepper, and Ellie stopped him. "I put pepper in yours already," she said. "Can't you see?"

He grunted. "Course I can see," he said. "Just want a little more, that's all." He sprinkled a little more pepper on and then set the shaker down.

Ellie felt somehow that she'd crossed him and felt bad about it. "Did you catch those digging cubs?" she asked.

He perked up, pleased that she'd remembered. "Nar," he said. "Can't tell how they got in neither."

"Are there...I didn't think there were walls or fences around the estate," Ellie said.

"Nar. But if they came from town, they came up on the road or they came through the field. But no tracks in the field, nor between the road and garden."

"What did they dig up this time?" Lorna was more outgoing when LeFou wasn't around.

"Can't tell. Ground's all torn up but weren't nothin' there to begin with." He scratched behind his ears. "Same spot as last time. Out of the way, might not've noticed it except I went back to t'winter shed for a heavy spade."

"Maybe the village boys made a treasure map," Lorna suggested.

Wilkins shook his head. "If I catch 'em, I'll give 'em a treasure."

Portia bounced into the room then, at a minute after seven. Ellie held out the plate of eggs and toast she'd made. "Ah, you're a dear," Portia said, and sat next to Wilkins at the small table in the servants' dining room. "What did you want to talk about?" she called, her mouth full of toast.

"Ah..." Ellie didn't want to bring up the money in front of the others. "It's a girl thing."

"I was married forty years," Wilkins said. "Heard it all. You go on."

Ellie fidgeted, and Portia, a veteran in the department of things people didn't want to talk about in front of other people, understood well enough. "I'll come in the kitchen," she said, bringing her plate.

Lorna was there, but she was on the other side of the kitchen, and Ellie didn't mind as much anyway if Lorna heard. "It's about the money you had yesterday," she said in a low voice.

"Don't worry about that," Portia said. "It's safe."

"No, I mean—" Ellie paused. "It seemed rather a lot."

"It was. My great-aunt died and left me some. I wasn't close to her, but sometimes people can surprise you."

Lorna turned around at this. "I thought you said last night you'd won a prize."

Portia's whiskered face scrunched up in annoyance. "Yes," she said, "I did say that, didn't I? I suppose I thought of it that way because I didn't really know her, so this money appeared from nowhere. But when I'd thought about it, I didn't think it was a very nice way to speak of a relative, even if I didn't know her well."

"Nice of her to leave you all that money," Ellie said.

"It isn't so very much. I had it in small notes, so it looks more than it is."

"All right. Well, I'm sorry for your great-aunt, but glad for you. What do you plan to do with it?"

"I told you last night. I'm going to London, have a nice night, maybe a weekend. I'm going to have some *fun* for a change."

Ellie clasped her paws together. "You're sure that money came from a great-aunt?" she asked, lowering her voice even further. "Because if you saw something, and you didn't go to the police with it..."

Portia's eyes widened for a moment, and then she shook her head and laughed. "Saw something? Whatever do you mean?"

Just then William entered the kitchen. He looked around, and then said to Portia, "The paring knife is still missing."

"I know," she said. "I'll get it in London tomorrow."

He exhaled. "All right," he said. "And the broom isn't in its proper place."

"Where is it?" Portia asked.

"I don't know. It isn't in its place."

"I'll help you find it." She heaved a sigh and squeezed Ellie's arm. "We can talk about this more tonight. But I'm alright, yeah?"

"Good," Ellie said.

Portia left with William, and Ellie and Lorna were left to carry on with making breakfast for the family. LeFou joined them at half-past and asked acerbically whether Ellie would be available for her duties for the entire day today. "I haven't been told otherwise," Ellie said, to underscore that it was Mister West who'd asked for her to run an errand.

"Good. Tonight we will be preparing a steak au poivre along with duchess potatoes and buttered beans. It is a simple recipe, but there are many places for it to go wrong." On this last word he looked at Lorna, who, though she was facing away from him, seemed to feel that the word was directed at her. Her shoulders hunched and her ears splayed, but she kept on with slicing the bread for toast.

"Yes, sir," Ellie said.

"By the way," he said, "you speak to Portia often, do you not?" When she nodded, he asked, "Have you noticed her with more money than usual?"

"Yes, sir." Ellie didn't hesitate. "Her great-aunt passed and left her a good sum, is what she told me."

"Is that so?" The fox rubbed his chin. "I suppose that

explains it. Now, let us see how your omelette skills have improved, if at all."

Ellie's omelette was passable, at least, if not complimented, and served to the family along with Lorna's toast and LeFou's sausages. Finley, as usual, was not present for breakfast, but Todd was, dressed in his suit jacket, and Ellie lingered in the servery to observe him.

He looked distressed, picking at his food and fidgeting with his silverware enough that Bonnie hissed across the table at him. Callie, sitting on the same side as Todd, looked over but did not say anything; she seemed determined not to let the recent murder affect the family. She spoke about a market in Groveby that she wanted to visit to look for antiques, and when none of the others responded to her questions about their plans for the day and week-end, carried on at length about other antiques she'd found there.

Beside her, James ate quietly and thoughtfully; across from him, Bonnie and Teddy both kept their heads down, though Teddy's ears were flat and Bonnie's were up.

The family was halfway through when Todd dropped one of his forks with a clatter on the floor. Callie stopped her story about the Victorian lamp and glared at him. Todd picked up the fork and then stood, still holding it. "I've got to catch the train," he said, and hurried out of the room, fork still clutched in one paw. The family watched him for a moment, and then Callie resumed her story as if nothing had happened.

When they'd finished eating, Mister West asked Ellie if she could join him in his study after lunch. "It won't take long, Laurent," the old badger said to LeFou, whose ears had flattened. "I promise, she will be available when you need to begin preparing supper."

"It does not matter to me one way or the other," LeFou said, "only you hire someone to be help in the kitchen and then you take them away from the kitchen. If you hire someone, they should remain in the kitchen."

The rest of the badgers around the table gaped or gasped at this impudence, but Mister West only smiled. "You must admit, Laurent, that these are extraordinary circumstances."

"I do not recognize extraordinary, as you say, circumstances, unless they mean that a meal is not required." The fox flicked his tail. "However, it shall be as you say. Miss Stone will see you after lunch and then will return promptly for supper."

"I will make sure of it," Mister West said.

* * *

Washing up after breakfast kept her busy, and then LeFou sent her down to the village for the things they would need for supper. Normally William would do this, but Ellie felt he was asserting his authority over her. So she walked down to see Gerald, whose niece had arrived to help him today, and picked up the vegetables she needed before walking down to the butcher's for steak, along with some mince for the staff supper. When she returned to Fortescue Hall, curious, she tried to spot the place where the cubs had been digging up the garden, but she couldn't spot it from the path, or else Wilkins had cleaned it up enough that it wasn't visible anymore.

LeFou cast an eye over her purchases and said nothing about them, which Ellie was beginning to realize was the best mark of approval she could hope for. She tied her apron on and set about preparing for lunch; there was to be a cold cucumber soup as well as small tartines of freshly-baked baguette.

A short time before lunch was due to be served, the kitchen door swung open and Callie strode in. She wore a simple, blue-checked dress with a silver brooch at the collar, a belt cinching her waist, and a felt hat with a small feather between her ears, every stitch precisely in place. Lorna, LeFou, and Ellie all looked up and snapped to attention, though LeFou kept slicing the cured ham he was preparing. "I'm here to speak to Miss Stone," Callie said in a crisp, sharp voice. "The rest of you may carry on."

They turned, Lorna hunched over the bread, LeFou keeping his ears cupped back toward the badger as she approached Ellie. "Miss Stone," she said. "We have not had much of a chance to acquaint ourselves. I have enjoyed your efforts in the kitchen and believe you have the potential to be an entirely acceptable cook. Perhaps even a good one."

"Thank you, ma'am," Ellie said.

"I do not know what compelled my brother to hire you here, but I feel comfortable in saying that his judgment was not amiss."

Ellie wasn't sure what to say to that. Another "thank you" seemed out of place, so she remained silent and let Callie go on. "But I am given to understand that he has ordered you to ask questions of the staff and townsfolk."

"Er, yes," Ellie said, aware of Lorna's and LeFou's eyes on her. "That's right."

"And what purpose do these questions serve?"

Ellie swallowed. "Has he not told you, ma'am?"

"I'm asking you," the badger said sharply.

"He...he asked me to ask questions about Georgette. The girl who was killed yesterday."

Callie kept her eyes fixed on Ellie. "Why?"

"He thinks that there may be more to her death. That he wants to understand."

"Of course he does." She drew in a breath. "Let me tell you something about my brother, Miss Stone. He's always been prone to flights of fancy. I won't deny that it's worked out for the best for him, through a stroke of luck that nobody could have foreseen. But he wasted good years of his life gallivanting around the world digging up things that should have stayed buried and making up stories about how they were used. The truth is, nobody knows for sure, and those people are all gone now."

Ellie thought archaeology was an interesting field, but she also didn't feel like having an argument with the stern, overbearing Callie. "Yes, ma'am," she said.

"My brother has finally left that life, and yet he is trying to re-create it wherever he can. He cares little whether the people around him have room for his fantasies in their lives. I cannot tell you to disobey him, but I would strongly advise you to limit the amount of energy you put into pursuing his..." She waved her paw. "Little dreams."

"Yes, ma'am. Thank you, ma'am," Ellie said.

Callie cast an eye down at the cucumber soup. "It looks like that needs more dill," she said, and swept out of the kitchen.

There was silence for a moment, as Ellie returned her attention to the soup, and then Lorna said, "Does he really think there was more to Georgette?"

"He does," Ellie said.

"And do you?" LeFou asked sharply.

"I...I do too," Ellie replied.

The silence in the kitchen dragged on for another few moments. And then LeFou said, "Perhaps there is. Perhaps there is not. It does not affect when lunch needs to be served."

"It won't," Ellie assured him. "Nor supper."

"See that it does not," he said, "but if that remains true, then for all I care you may go down to the graveyard and dig up her body."

Ellie's tail curled in against her hip. But she accepted the permission—and the tacit rebuttal of Callie's argument—in the spirit in which it was given, even with LeFou's gruesome example. "I don't think there will be need for that," she said.

At lunch, the whole family except for Finley was present, Todd having come back from London on the midday train.

They seemed to have recovered their spirits; at least, the older ones had. Callie and James both tried to make Todd's first week of work at the bank a topic of conversation, but the young badger said only that he was glad it was over and, "I'm not sure it's for me." When pressed, he wouldn't elaborate (though at least he did not drop any more silverware), and eventually Callie moved on to telling Bonnie about the young noble who was going to come visit that Sunday, the son of a count or an earl (she wasn't sure). This received a frosty reception, until Mister West intervened to say that of course Bonnie understood what was expected of her, she'd been through it a hundred times, and Callie responded sharply that if Bonnie understood what was expected of her, she'd be married by now, and at that Bonnie got up and left the table.

"Now see what you've done," Callie said to her brother.

"If you understood people half as well as you understand society," Mister West replied, "you wouldn't be putting yourself and your daughter in these situations."

"I'm looking out for her well-being!" Callie exclaimed. "She just doesn't appreciate that, and Charles, I lay that at your door."

"You're right, dear. I'll talk to her."

"Perhaps she'll listen to you." Callie sniffed. "No time to spend one afternoon with a pleasant young badger, and do you know how many calls I had to make to arrange this visit? But she can go off for a month to visit friends."

"It's an important gathering," Mister West said. "As I understand it."

"You needn't rub my nose in how much better you understand my children than I do," Callie said with more than a tinge of bitterness.

Ellie helped Lorna clean up when the lunch was done and then made her way to Mr. West's study. When she knocked on the door, he called out, "Just a moment."

So Ellie waited in the hallway, and after a few minutes, the door opened and Bonnie came out. She did not acknowledge Ellie but swept past her and away down the hallway. "Come on in, Miss Stone," Mister West called from inside the study.

He still wore the brown tweed suit he'd had on at lunch, but without the tie. He waved her to one of the two chairs in front of his desk, and she chose the one that did not sit in the sunlight streaming in from the large windows. "Now," he said, "what have you discovered?"

"I talked to Gerald at the greengrocer's," Ellie said, "to Mrs. Chatcombe, who let her rooms, and to Betsy, Georgette's friend who runs the magazine stand outside the station, and they all said she was seeing someone here, but they thought she was about to end it. She seemed angry about it. Betsy said it was Teddy, but the others didn't know for sure."

He nodded. "What did Portia have to say about it?"

"Well." Ellie weighed her new friend's trust against the investigation and tried to thread that needle. After all, Portia had been bragging about her money, so it wasn't exactly a secret. "She says she's come into money recently."

"I heard." The badger laced his fingers together and rested the grey of his muzzle atop them, studying her.

"She's been a little strange about the money, and about the thing she saw around the murder yesterday. I think she knows something and blackmailed whoever it was."

He nodded. "So it wasn't Devon. And it was likely one of the family. I wonder how much money Miss Davis has...no." He sighed heavily. "Bless Devon for trying to cover it up."

This seemed an odd thing to say about someone who had at the very least committed the crime of interfering with a police investigation, but Ellie understood where it was coming from. She changed the subject delicately. "And Portia says Todd has been acting strange ever since her death. Georgette's, I mean."

"I noticed this morning," Mister West said. "Does she know why? Do you?"

Ellie shook her head. "But from what Portia said, I don't think Todd killed her. He seems more distraught over her death than Teddy does, come to that."

"He did." Mister West chuckled. "I wonder if he took that fork all the way to London or left it on the train."

The chuckle felt a little wrong to Ellie, but she passed over it. "Oh, and it does seem like Finley might have been here," she said. "He came in on the 5:38 train yesterday as you suspected, went over to the Somerleyton Pint, and then disappeared. And Portia was over there, too. That's where I first saw her with the money." She told him about the warehouse Betsy had explained to her, how Portia had been there with someone else.

"Hm," Mister West said. "It's possible. I know he'd been meeting someone. LeFou said it was a hedgehog, but that could have been a cover. Did you see a hedgehog at the pub?"

Ellie thought about the other patrons. "No. Gerald is a hedgehog, but he's the only one I saw yesterday."

"Well. It's something to keep in mind. I suspect our next step should be for me to bring Portia in here. What do you think?"

"She won't like it," Ellie said. "But I agree. I think—" She stopped. "Did you hear that?"

Mister West frowned. "I did not. What?"

"There was a scream."

CHAPTER 14
THE GARDEN TOWER

Mister West stood quickly. "Let us investigate," he said, "although I am certain we will know what's happened before long."

Ellie stood too, although her heart felt heavy and she suspected she already knew what had happened.

The old badger moved surprisingly quickly for his age, but Ellie still chafed to run ahead of him as they moved down the front hallway to where it met the west corridor. There she paused and listened again, and this time they both heard a wailing coming from the west corridor. "This way," Ellie said, and Mister West followed her.

"Someone help!" came a cry, and when Ellie turned from the west corridor into the back hallway, she saw one of the housemaids she didn't know well, a young dhole, standing in the doorway of the patio room and looking into it.

"We're here," called Mister West, and the dhole turned toward them just as Miss Davis turned the corner from the east corridor, closer to her.

"What is this commotion about?" the rabbit asked sternly. "Marigold, you know that if there's a problem, you come and find me quietly."

"There." The dhole pointed with a shaky finger into the patio room.

Miss Davis stood and stared. "There's nothing in the room," she said. "Girl, are you seeing spirits?"

Ellie and Mister West had reached the big double doors that led out to the garden, just feet from the patio room door, when the dhole said, "Ou-outside, mum."

And Miss Davis, still cross, looked again and this time brought her paws to her muzzle and gasped aloud. Ellie could not keep herself from hurrying the last few steps ahead of Mister West, and when she reached the doorway and looked through the room to the window, she saw outside on the garden patio the body of Portia, draped lifeless across the railing.

"It's Portia," she said, turning to Mister West as he joined them.

"She m-must have jumped," the dhole said, still shakily.

Miss Davis put a paw on her shoulder. "Marigold, go and get a cup of tea from Lorna and sit in your room. You're excused from your duties the rest of the day."

"Thank you, mum."

The rabbit didn't release her shoulder. "And don't say a word of this to anyone. Mister West is here and he'll take charge of the situation. We don't need a lot of people back here gawking."

"Yes'm." And Marigold took off for the kitchen, her tail curled between her legs.

"Ma'am," Ellie said, "how does one get to the roof?"

"The roof?" Miss Davis shook her head. "You can't walk about on the roof. Do you mean the garden tower?"

"Yes." Ellie stifled her impatience. "It's just over the Garden View room, isn't it? Is there a stair from there?"

Mister West interrupted. "I know the way," he said. "I'll take you. Mildred, please ring the constable and alert him to the situation. And if you can keep people away from here as you've been doing, it would be much appreciated. Use the phone in the patio room here."

"Yes, sir," Miss Davis said, and moved to the patio room. "I'll keep an eye for Wilkins as well."

"Good lady." Mister West turned his attention to Ellie. "This way."

He led her up the east stairs to the second floor and then opened a door off the back hallway that Ellie had never seen open. A spiral stair lay beyond it, stone, and Mister West climbed it with Ellie close behind him. "I don't believe she jumped," Ellie said as she climbed. "I suppose people can have hidden depths, but...she had plans. She was excited about the future."

"I didn't talk to her much," Mister West panted ahead of her. "I will trust your judgment on this. If she was blackmailing someone, as you suggest, then..." He didn't finish. He didn't need to.

The stair continued past the third story room—the third floor, Ellie was given to understand, was not used, as the space was not needed, and consequently the third floor air felt warm and stuffy. Nevertheless, there lingered a scent of badger in it, and none of otter that she could detect, all the way up to a door which Mister West tried and found unlocked.

"Wait," Ellie called as he opened it. "Don't disturb the scene."

He smiled down at her. "I wasn't going to, sergeant. But thank you for the reminder."

She came up to stand alongside him at the door, and the two of them looked out at the top of the garden tower. The sun beat down on Ellie's fur, and the air here was warmer than inside, if not as stuffy. No breeze moved.

The whole area was about twenty feet square, surrounded by a balustrade of white stone. A light coating of dirt lay over everything, residue of rain and wind, undisturbed except by a trail of indistinct footprints leading out to the far side of the tower, the side overlooking the garden. And there, where the footprints ended, a piece of paper lay under a small rock on the balustrade. Ellie pointed to it, and Mister West nodded, his eyes bright and alert. "I see it," he said. "We are meant to think she jumped from here. What do you make of this?"

His paw swept out, indicating the tile between here and there. Ellie looked and then crouched to get closer. "I don't smell Portia, but...the scent up here would be faint anyway. There's only one set of tracks I can see...they do seem to go out and not come back. But..." She drew a finger across the tile, then stood again and shaded her eyes. "It's dirty up here. Doesn't get cleaned."

"That's why we can see tracks," Mister West agreed.

She had the feeling that he had already noticed something and was waiting for her to notice it too. Testing her, perhaps. Or perhaps he was relying on her observation. "I don't see any tracks on the balustrade, is the thing."

His muzzle swung out to look toward the note again. "On the balustrade?"

"She would have climbed up on it, wouldn't she? If she'd jumped? She wouldn't have placed the note and then...leapt over the balustrade. So there should be dirty footprints on the white. But I don't see any."

Mister West narrowed his eyes. "It's hard to tell, but...nor do I, I think." He gestured to his right. "Let's go over there. Keep to the edge so we don't disturb the tracks."

She nodded and stepped carefully, following the balustrade around the little rooftop. The tile heated her paws, and she could feel the grit and dust scrape with every step. When they reached the front of the tower, she glanced over and saw Portia's body still draped across the patio, and her heart tightened with grief, thinking about all the plans the otter had had and would never get to carry out now. No night in London with a handsome fellow, no fancy dinner followed by a theater show, no new dress, no new curtains. She looked away and drew in a breath. Catch the one who did this, she told herself. That's what you can do for her now.

They reached the note finally, gleaming white paper on the dirty white balustrade, and Ellie pointed to the stone around the paper. "No footprints up here."

"No," Mister West agreed. "What does the paper say?"

"I'm sure it says…" Ellie reached out to pick it up. "I'm sorry, goodbye, something like that." She picked it up and held it out to him. "You see? 'Very sorry. I will miss all of you, but I must do this.'"

"Part of another note." He drew his claw along the bottom edge. "It's torn here."

Ellie nodded. "She was thinking about leaving. I shouldn't be surprised if that's what she meant to be writing about."

"It is her writing, then?" Mister West asked.

Ellie didn't answer right away. The tile in front of the balustrade showed two footmarks, probably larger than Portia's feet, but smudged, not provably larger. But next to them was a round imprint, as though a coin had been lying there and been picked up.

"Sergeant?" Mister West said playfully, and then, when Ellie still didn't answer, putting together things in her head, he lost the playful tone. "Miss Stone."

"I'm sorry," she said. "I think it's Portia's writing, although I haven't seen very much of it."

"What are you staring at?"

She pointed. "There. Next to the footprint. You see it?"

He held onto her arm and leaned over slightly. "I think so. It's…"

"It's the answer," she said.

Mister West straightened but kept hold of her arm. "Tell me," he said gently.

"It's Teddy," she said. "Of course it is. The cane, that was the thing. He hit Georgette with his cane, not the poker. I knew there was something wrong about the fireplace, but I focused on the wrong thing."

The old badger's eyes were bright in the sun. "What was wrong about the fireplace?"

"The poker. The poker was lying in the fireplace. That was wrong. Georgette fell in front of the fireplace, and if someone had killed her with the poker, like Devon said, they wouldn't have placed it carefully in the ashes afterwards. They'd have dropped it on the carpet or flung it into the fireplace—but there weren't ashes scattered around, like there would be then. They were in a neat pile."

"Then why put the poker there?"

"To hide the fact that it hadn't been used. He should have pressed it to her head—maybe he did—but if there were an investigation, there wasn't blood and hair on the poker. If he put it in the ashes, there'd be contamination and maybe it would be inconclusive."

"I'm not sure that would have worked."

"No," Ellie agreed, "but that was about his intention, not about what would have worked. He wanted to dirty up the poker so it wouldn't be clearly *not* the murder weapon. Because the murder weapon was being washed off in the fountain." She stared out at the garden. "The fountain..."

"And he knew Wilkins takes his lunch and stays inside in the heat of midday," Mister West went on. "So he could kill Portia in the Garden View Room and then come up here to place the note."

"There is someone out there, though." Ellie pointed to the far corner of the garden, where a figure moved furtively. It looked like a badger carrying a shovel, though at this distance she couldn't tell any more about it.

"That's not Teddy," Mister West said. "He's somewhere else by now."

The train of thought that had started with the fountain jerked back to life in Ellie's mind. "He's going to Portia's room," she said. "I'm sorry, I have to hurry before he finds it."

"Go," Mister West told her. "I'll follow."

CHAPTER 15
THE LARGER SERVANTS ROOM

Ellie hurried around the edge of the terrace and down the spiral stairs to the second floor, past the gentlemen's chambers where Todd, Teddy, and Finley lived. The door to the servants' quarters stood ajar, and she pushed through it, heart pounding. If she were too late, they might lose the only piece of real evidence they had—if her speculation was right.

The servants' quarters should all be empty this time of day, and they were, until Ellie burst into her own room and found Lavinia sitting on the bed with her pad, but she wasn't drawing.

The rabbit sat up with a start and dropped the pad. A letter and envelope fell off it onto the bed. "Ellie! You frightened me."

"How long have you been here?" Ellie stared at the door to Portia's room.

Lavinia gathered up the letter and envelope, slid them into the pad, and set it down. "Did Mother send you up here?"

"No." Ellie wanted to ask Lavinia about the envelope, but there was a more pressing matter. She crossed the room and looked into Portia's. It was empty, and there was no smell of badger that she could detect, not like there had been out in the hallways. "It's very important. Have you been here since lunch?"

The rabbit hesitated and then nodded. "I know I'm meant to be airing out the bedrooms, but...sometimes I come back here to sketch. I can do them later. After lunch, I don't feel like working so much."

"It's fine," Ellie said. "It's excellent, even. Did anyone come by trying to get in?"

"Now how would you know that?" Lavinia picked up her pad and pencil. "I thought Mother came by to look for me, but there was a strange thumping noise with it. I stayed very quiet and they went away."

"A thumping noise." Ellie's heart was slowing down. "Like someone using a cane."

"It might have been." Lavinia hunched up a little more, the pad against her knees. "I didn't see. Sometimes Mother does come here looking for me, but it wasn't her."

"All right." Ellie leaned against the door frame. "Can you do something for me? It's very important."

The rabbit's eyes widened and she looked up. "I don't know if I can promise that until I hear what it is."

"I just need you to stay here. Make sure nobody goes into Portia's room. I'll arrange it with your mother."

Lavinia laughed. "You'll arrange it with Mother. Have you been promoted, then?"

"In a manner of speaking." Ellie crossed to the bed and sat on it, putting one paw on Lavinia's knee. "Portia's dead. They say she jumped, but—"

"She never!" Lavinia's shock interrupted Ellie.

"No. I don't think so, and Mister West doesn't either. But she had something that the murderer wants, and I think I know what it is, but we have to leave it there for the moment. Mister West will be here shortly."

"Mister West!"

"That's how we'll arrange it with your mother." Ellie patted her knee and got up.

Lavinia watched her as she crossed to Portia's room to look inside. "What is it that's in there? Is it all the money she had?"

"That's part of it."

Before Ellie could go on, Mister West arrived. He leaned against the doorframe, panting a little, but his eyes remained sharp and fixed on Ellie. "Did he get to it?"

"No. Lavinia's been here since lunch. She thinks she heard him in the hallway, but he didn't come in."

"Good girl," Mister West said.

"I've asked if she can stay here for the rest of the afternoon. Will you talk to Miss Davis about it?"

"Of course." His eyes flicked to Portia's room. "Are you sure it's still there? And what is it?"

"I haven't looked, but...he wouldn't have come to get it before lunch, would he? He'd come by after he'd..." She looked toward the garden and ducked her head.

"Would he not have asked her to bring it to their meeting?" Mister West asked.

Ellie hesitated. "Perhaps," she said slowly, "but if it's what I think it is, then that wouldn't really make much sense."

"And I did hear someone with a cane coming along the hallway," Lavinia put in. "But he stopped."

Mister West nodded slowly. "All right," he said. "I will talk to Miss Davis. And I would like you, Miss Stone, to talk to the constable when he arrives."

"Me?" Ellie blinked. "Why me?"

The old badger smiled sadly. "You have been here less than a week, and so you are not privy to all the tensions and stresses at play here. It does not matter if my great-nephew is a murderer; in the interest of family peace, I cannot be the one to turn him in. Callie already resents having to live under my roof, even though she and her family have always been welcome here. To add another resentment to the pile..." He pressed his paws together and looked down at them. "They would move somewhere else, where they would live in hardship, and I would have to live alone. With their hardship weighing on my mind. And already, there is going to be..." He broke off and waved a paw, looking up. "That is not your concern. But you will note that I am not ordering you to do this. I am asking, as a favor to an old badger who is trying to keep the peace in his home."

Ellie took in a breath. "Of course I will do it. But if it's to be me..."

"It must be you."

She nodded. Lavinia watched her, eyes wide. "I do not have a lot of confidence in this constable," she said.

"Understandable," Mister West said dryly. "I presume from your past experience that there is someone you have more confidence in."

Her heart speeded up. "There is. He's a sergeant who investigated the other murders I—that is, the murders that took place where I was employed. I trust him a great deal. May I ring him up and ask him to come?"

"Of course you may. Use the phone in my study. How long will it take him to get here?"

"If he's available, it shouldn't be more than an hour." Her tail flicked. She was genuinely looking forward to seeing Sergeant Cooke again, even with the chance he might ask her out.

Mister West nodded. "And when he gets here, what then?"

"Well, I've been thinking about that." Ellie looked around the room. "If there was a room here at Fortescue where one might observe people in it without being seen, we could move Portia's things into that room and say that her family were going to come pick them up."

"And catch him as he comes to take it."

"Or we could leave them there and station someone in the next room—is that Marigold's? And catch him as he leaves."

Mister West nodded and then rubbed his chin, turning over something in his head. Finally he spoke. "I'm somewhat embarrassed to tell you that we may leave Portia's things in her room. When this manor was built, the lord had passages put in so he might spy on the servants. We have never used them, of course, but they exist."

"What?" Lavinia exclaimed. "All the servant rooms?"

"I'm afraid so." The old badger pressed his paws together again. "The cupboards along this hallway, for example, we have turned into linen cupboards, but the backs are secret doors that open."

"That's horrible," Lavinia said, and after a beat remembered to add, "sir."

"Clearly," Mister West said, more annoyed, "which is why we turned those doors into linen cupboards and haven't ever opened them."

"No, I mean..." The rabbit stopped, confused. "I didn't mean you, sir. I meant the people who built it."

"Yes, and the people who used it," Mister West said, "but it had already been closed off when Father bought the house. So I presume it hadn't been used in some time. But the owners did take pains to show it to us when we made the sale. They thought we might be interested, I suppose."

"Does Mother know about this?" Lavinia asked.

Mister West shifted from one foot to the other. "Nobody else knows about it. Except the fellow who put the shelves in, I suppose, but Lester retired from carpentry years ago. I don't suppose he's mentioned it to anyone."

"Where are the...the peep-holes?" Ellie examined the wall opposite the windows.

"Let's address that in a little bit," Mister West said. "Come with me, Ellie. I have to speak to Miss Davis, and you have a phone call to make from my study."

"I'll catch up with you in a moment, sir, if I may," Ellie said, looking down at Lavinia on the bed.

The old badger looked back at her. "If you think it best, sergeant," he said, and stepped out of the room.

"'Sergeant'?" Lavinia said faintly.

"It's a game of his." Ellie sat down on her bed. "He likes to solve puzzles. He's a detective and I'm a sergeant in his game."

"I suppose that makes sense."

"Only it isn't a game," Ellie said. She listened but could not hear Mister West's footsteps anywhere outside. "I only wanted to ask about that envelope. Did you get it from Georgette yesterday?" When Lavinia hesitated, Ellie continued. "I won't tell your mother. It's something to do with your art, isn't it? Are you showing at a gallery somewhere?"

Lavinia laughed, and the tension drained out of her. "Bless you, no, I'm not that good yet. But it is...yes, it's about that. Promise you won't tell Mother?"

"I promise."

"I'm going to art school." She reached into the pad and pulled out the envelope. "This was the letter telling me I was accepted. They're going to pay for some of my tuition, but I'll have to work for the rest of it. I don't suppose Mother will help me at all."

Ellie nodded. "Mister West might, if you ask him."

Lavinia's eyes widened. "Do you think so?"

Ellie stood. "I think it likely. Only ask him directly, because he likely won't want your mother to know. Anything to not upset the peace of the house." She smiled. "That's wonderful. I'm so glad for you, and I can't wait to hear more about it, only I have to..." She gestured to the door.

"Solve a murder, I know." Lavinia tucked the paper back

into the pad. "Is it Teddy, then? Mister West said it was his great-nephew, and I heard the cane."

Ellie hesitated and then nodded. "We think so. But you can't tell anyone."

The rabbit shook her head, but fearfully. "To think! I was lying here and he was just outside. He might've done anything." She gulped. "You don't think he'll try to come back? When he finds out the constable is coming?"

Ellie put a paw on her knee, the gesture of comforting a rabbit very familiar. "We'll keep watch on him, now we know. I promise I won't let anything happen to you."

"All right." Lavinia smiled. "Thank you, Ellie. But if I see Teddy, I shall scream as loud as I can."

"And we'll come running. But you won't see him, and it won't be long now." Ellie patted the rabbit's knee and left the room.

CHAPTER 16
THE LARGE PARLOUR

Sergeant Cooke was very pleased to hear from her, even given the circumstances, and the wolf promised to drop everything and hurry up to Willow's End. Ellie hung up with a wash of relief that he hadn't been put off by her silence the last few months. When she emerged back into the front hall, a clamor of voices came from the large parlor. Ellie rounded the corner of the hall and looked through the door to see the whole family (save for Finley), seated on couches and chairs, and most of the staff standing in one corner of the study behind Miss Davis, who was comforting the dhole housemaid. Only Lavinia was absent.

Mister West was addressing them. "...all take some time to come to terms with this tragedy while we wait for the police to arrive." He spotted her at the door. "Ah, Miss Stone, please come in. Where have you been?"

The stares of the family felt icy on Ellie's fur. "I've been making a phone call," she said, and then stopped herself from saying, "as you told me to."

"To whom?" Mister West asked.

Ellie's mouth and throat felt dry. "As a few of you might know, there was a murder at a house where I was working. This was two years ago. But the sergeant on the case was clever, and he and I got along well, so I asked if he might have a chance to come down here just in case there was something the local police missed."

"A murder?" Mister West looked surprised. "But surely Portia simply jumped, poor girl? There was a note."

"Of course." Ellie was a little put off by how much Mister West seemed to be enjoying his performance. Portia was dead, and Georgette too. Of course he had to keep peace in his house, but...she set that aside. "But in Portia's case, she was so important to us...I'm sorry if I overstepped." She had the sense of being in a play where she hadn't been told any of her lines, and where the audience was not enjoying it at all. "I can try to call back, but he said he'd leave right away."

"You have overstepped," Mister West said, "but there's nothing to be done about it now. When our Constable Partridge arrives, we will tell him there is a senior officer on the way as well so that he knows not to touch anything."

"We aren't to touch anything?" William asked. "Anywhere?" Lorna touched his arm and said something to him. "But I haven't been in those rooms," he said. "How could I have—" She whispered to him again.

Callie stood, ignoring William. "This is ridiculous," she said. "The poor girl was disturbed and took a foolish step. There's no reason the rest of us should be inconvenienced by it."

"Callie," James said, setting a paw on her arm. "Have a heart. Remember back in Paris when there was that robbery? They wanted us all in one place to—"

"I have a heart," she snapped. "I care about our children, and their children, sitting in this stuffy room fretting about a girl who did not care a whit for any of them."

"Here now," Bonnie said. "Portia was a dear."

"A dear busybody, you mean," Todd put in. He'd stood up

when his grandmother had and now paced anxiously in front of the couch. "Who here hasn't left a room quickly and found her listening right around the corner? She was in everyone's business. She knew things and she'd tell them to anyone." He wrung his paws together.

"Actually." Ellie cleared her throat, now drier than ever.

The family ignored her. "Servants are meant to listen at doors," Bonnie said. She took a sip from the glass of water next to her while Ellie looked on enviously. "Everyone knows that. If you don't, you deserve whatever came of it."

"Nothing 'came of it,'" Todd said hotly, rounding on her. "What does that mean? What did she tell you?"

"It is not seemly," Callie said, "and it reflects poorly on the staff." Here she stared at Miss Davis.

The rabbit seemed taken aback by this unexpected attack. "I—I told her not to—I cannot be watching her every moment. But she's gone now, poor thing, and—"

"What did she tell you?" Todd turned to Miss Davis when Bonnie ignored him. "What did she say?"

Ellie tried clearing her throat again, to no effect as the badgers all turned on Miss Davis, putting her in the unfortunate position of having to defend Portia out of a desire not to speak ill of the dead while clearly agreeing with all the attacks leveled against the departed otter.

Mister West put his paws up, and in a deep voice said, "Enough!" He had to say it again before the family quieted and grudgingly acknowledged him. "Miss Stone has something else to say to us."

"Yes," Ellie said. "Thank you. The sergeant asked that everyone be kept away from—that is, in one place until he can arrive and talk to them. To us, to all of us. He said it is standard procedure."

Callie turned her withering glare on Ellie. "'Standard procedure' for what? Nothing about this is 'standard.'"

"As I was saying—" her husband began, but stopped when she slapped his paw away from her arm.

Miss Davis chimed in, glad to be on the attack now. "This is highly irregular. Are we all suspects? What does this mean?"

A general clamor went up until Mister West raised his paws again. "It is only an hour," he said. "If the police have requested it, I think we'd better follow their instructions. It will make things easier in the long run."

Ellie watched Teddy, sitting on the couch next to Bonnie. He fidgeted but didn't look directly at her or his great-uncle. Mister West didn't look at him either, addressing Ellie next. "Ellie, go see if Lavinia is feeling better, and have her join us if she is." At that, Teddy's ears did flick, but he didn't otherwise react.

Todd, however, did. "Why does she get to leave?" he demanded. "What if *she* goes and mucks about on the roof or the patio or whatever the police want us to leave alone? I wager she's going to go through our rooms. Well, go ahead! You'll find nothing in mine. Ha ha!" His laugh sounded shaky.

"Miss Stone is not going to search anyone's room. That is the police's job," Mister West said smoothly. "But Miss Stone has experience in crime scenes. She would hardly have called an investigator if she were involved in the murder. Besides which, she was in the kitchen during and after lunch, and then came directly to my study, as several people can attest."

"As I was also in the kitchen after lunch, and indeed until you came and dragged us all here," LeFou said, "may I be permitted to return to the kitchen so I may begin the preparations for supper? I trust there is nothing of interest to the police in my kitchen or my rooms, and I have no interest in stepping anywhere near the roof or garden."

"Oh, let him go back to the kitchen, or else he'll pout and skip dinner again," Callie said.

Ellie felt the sting of that—she'd managed dinner well, and

it had been mostly LeFou's cooking anyway—but she kept quiet. LeFou did not, but his protest followed different lines. "I do not 'pout,'" he said stiffly. "I take pride in my work. If I am forced to a place where I cannot do my best work, I would prefer not to do the work at all."

"Supper still must be served." Callie's tone sharpened. "Isn't that your job?"

Miss Davis, clearly trying to make the peace, said, "Miss Stone is evidently in a trusted position. Can she not begin the preparations? And then, Mr. LeFou, we will ensure you are questioned first, so you may be released to the kitchen."

The fox considered this and then turned to Ellie with a not-very-nice smile. "There are five pounds of potatoes in the larder. They must be peeled and diced. There is a bag of pepper on the counter next to the stove. It must be crushed. Do you understand?"

"Yes, sir," Ellie said. She knew that steak au poivre was a quick recipe, if not simple, and that LeFou would not have peeled the potatoes himself in any case. But it was part of the dinner preparation, and she was an assistant cook, so she couldn't very well refuse to do her job.

"I still don't understand why she's allowed to leave," Todd said. "Do you trust her more than your own family? And why do you keep saying 'murder'? The poor daft girl jumped."

"Do sit down, Todd. You're making things worse," Bonnie said. And then, as her nephew did so, she added, "Besides, maybe the poor girl was pushed."

That set off another clamor of frustrating shouting. Ellie took advantage of the distraction to leave the squabbling family and went back first to her room, where Lavinia still sat on the bed. "I sketched Portia," she said. "Or I tried. I'm afraid I didn't quite do her justice."

She showed Ellie, and for a moment Ellie couldn't speak. Technically, Lavinia might be an amateur, but her drawing had captured something of Portia, the life that had been in the otter, her mouth open and eyes wide, happily telling anyone anything. She swallowed and then said, "I think it's lovely. Really."

"It's not finished, but you can see...oh, dear. It just hit me sitting here after you left that she won't be coming through that door to bother us anymore, and...would you mind terribly if I put this up in the room? I can wait until you leave if you'd rather."

"It won't bother me at all. But leave it for now. We have to open that secret passage, and then you're to come to the parlor with everyone else. The constable will be here shortly, and the sergeant soon after that."

"The sergeant?" Lavinia blinked at her. "There isn't a sergeant in our police station."

"I called a friend of mine."

"You're friends with a police sergeant?"

Ellie nodded. "He came to advise on the first murder—well, murders—a few years ago, and then he called me to look at the second one—well, actually, Abby called me, but the Sergeant came along as the official investigator."

Lavinia frowned and then stood. She looked down at the picture of Portia on the bed. "If someone did kill her, then I'm glad for any help finding who did it. Are you sure her things, or whatever thing it was you wanted to protect, will be safe?"

"I'm sure. Mister West knows not to let him out of the room until we're ready." She looked at the wall but still could not see where the peepholes were.

"We? You and me?"

"No, me and—well, one of the policemen. Or maybe Mister West. I'm not certain yet."

They left the room and opened the linen cupboard. Lavinia showed Ellie another cupboard down the hall where the linens could be moved, and then they worked at the shelves. They had not been secured down, but had been fitted well to the cupboard, so it was some work to lift them away from the brackets they'd been resting on.

"I feel worried that they come off so easily," Lavinia said as they leaned the shelves against the cupboard wall. "Has he been using this passage in the past?"

Ellie sniffed at the back, feeling along it for some latch or lever. "I don't think so. It just smells of linen in here. No badger smell. Ah." The left side, not the right, pushed inward with a scraping, revealing a space full of dust and spiderwebs. "Eugh. Nobody's been back here in years. Decades, maybe."

Lavinia retreated. "I don't like spiders," she said. "Close it up."

Ellie left the inner door open but stepped out of the linen cupboard and closed it. "There," she said. "Unless he comes looking for linens, he won't notice anything."

"Let's go." Lavinia stared at the bottom of the cupboard door as though worried spiders would come streaming out of it.

By the time they reached the parlor, the red deer constable had already arrived. He was talking to Mister West in the doorway, sounding put out. When he spotted Ellie, he shifted his attention to her and ignored Lavinia, who slipped past them. "And here's the problem herself. Out-of-towner come in here, and the local constabulary isn't good enough for her, is it? Got to call some fancy sergeant. Let me tell you, young miss, I've seen deaths in this village. Filled out the reports all by myself, I did. Didn't need any fancy sergeant from London to tell me what's what."

"He's not from London—" Ellie said.

"Think he knows the people in this village better'n what I do? Think he knows who could be a murderer? I know." He jabbed his own chest with a finger.

"All right," Mister West said hastily, as behind him more of the badgers were taking notice of the red deer's loud voice. "It's done, and we can't help it now."

"You can tell that sergeant when he arrives that he en't needed."

"I have kitchen work to do," Ellie said, and hurried away back to the kitchen.

CHAPTER 17
THE SECRET PASSAGE

She found the potatoes, then realized that there was nobody to greet Sergeant Cooke when he arrived. So she dragged the heavy sack and a pot out to the front doorstep and sat there in the summer afternoon heat, peeling potatoes, and that's how the Sergeant found her when he drove up twenty minutes later in a small beige car with an unlit red light on the top.

He slowed at the circular driveway and then pulled up to the door, where he got out and stood while Ellie picked up the pot with the peeled potatoes in it. "I can get that for you, if you like," the wolf said with a smile.

"I've got the pot, but if you could get the ones I haven't peeled yet, that would be a help." She had picked up the pot so that he wouldn't try to hug her, but she couldn't stop him from leaning in and touching muzzles. "It's nice to see you again. Thanks for coming."

"You didn't have to wait for a suspicious death to call me," he said lightly, picking up the sack in one paw. "But I did not expect to find you peeling potatoes."

"I'm an assistant cook, and there's work to do," she replied, showing him into the entryway and then into the front hall.

"We'll just put these in the kitchen while I explain to you what's been happening."

So as they walked through the dining room and servery into the kitchen, she told him about Georgette's death and how Devon had taken responsibility for it, how it had felt strange to her and Mister West both, how Portia had seen something strange and then made up the story about the bird, how she'd then had a good deal of money and had supposedly jumped to her death from a balustrade that didn't have any footprints or marks on it.

"And I think," she said, setting the pot on the counter and pointing to the space beside it for the sack, "that she was blackmailing Teddy. He came to our room straight away when he'd killed her, looking for something, except Lavinia was there and so he couldn't get in to get it. At least," she caught herself, "someone with a cane or walking-stick did. But all the evidence points to Teddy. Mister MacTavish also uses a stick but he's in his seventies and I don't think he could've climbed to the tower that quickly. So we've gathered everyone in the parlor. We want you to question Teddy first and then release him so he thinks he can come to the room and get it, and we've a way to watch the room." She took a breath as Sergeant Cooke sat the sack next to the pot, watching her. "So you can catch him in the act."

"I think I've got all that," the wolf said. "Only how am I meant to catch him if I'm also questioning people?"

"Oh." Ellie stopped. "Well...the local constable is here, and he's not happy about me calling you. I suppose he could conduct the interviews if you instruct him."

Cooke nodded. "Easy enough to do. 'Wouldn't want to get in the way of the local police, you know these people best,' and so on. I can do that." He put a paw on Ellie's arm as she turned to leave the kitchen. "And what do you think Teddy's looking for in Portia's room?"

"Well. One of two things. Maybe both. That is, I think both

are in Portia's room, but he might only be looking for one or the other. The one thing is easy: the money he paid her as blackmail. It's in her handbag. The other—" Ellie paused. Saying it aloud committed her to the belief, and if she was wrong...but she was pretty sure about it. "He was wearing a jacket the day Georgette was killed, and he came in from the garden with it all wet. He said he'd fallen in the fountain. But that was when Portia said she'd seen something strange in the garden, and I think it was probably Teddy standing in it or washing his jacket in it or something. He had to clean off his cane, but he wouldn't have had to get his jacket wet for that. Just dip it in the fountain."

"But you think the jacket had blood on it."

She nodded. "I think he didn't mean to kill Georgette. She just made him mad. And when she fell down and wasn't moving, he tried to revive her or hold her and got blood on his jacket. And Portia said she has to clean Teddy's clothes now that Devon's gone to jail. I don't think Teddy thought about it, but she went and got the jacket and other clothes from his room, and she must have realized there was something about the jacket. It probably smelled of blood; I'm sure he couldn't have gotten all of it out. But he wasn't thinking that he had to, because faithful Devon would take care of it. So I think Portia never washed the jacket and it's still in her room."

"Did you check?" Cooke asked.

Ellie rubbed her paws together. They felt gritty from the potatoes. "I didn't want to disturb anything."

"I'm an officer. Let's make sure these things are where you think we are before we lay a trap with them, shall we?"

Ellie nodded. "That makes sense. Thank you."

As she led him up the dining hall stairs and then around the corridors that led to the servants' quarters, she said, "I'm glad you're here. Mister West wanted to investigate this death and then it turned out there really was something funny going on about it, but I didn't feel right doing any of this without a real police officer around."

"You've done very well." Cooke rested a paw on her shoulder and then removed it almost immediately. "I wish every case began with someone having identified the suspect for me and providing a means to ensure their guilt."

"You can arrest him, then? If we find the jacket?"

"I'd like to examine the rooftop before we go down to the parlour, as that's the fresher crime scene," the wolf said. "But if all is as you say it is—and I have no reason to doubt it will be—then I think we can reasonably make an arrest."

They arrived in Portia's room, and Ellie confirmed again that it had not been disturbed since her death; there were no scents but hers. "Let me handle everything," Cooke instructed, "but you can tell me where to look."

"All right." Ellie scanned the room. Portia's scent was strong in here and it brought back the memories of talking to her in the pub, sitting on their bed together, seeing her body lying broken on the patio. She steadied herself. "Try the chest of drawers first and then perhaps...under the bed?"

The jacket turned up at the back of the bottom drawer. Sergeant Cooke reached back and said, "Ah, a military jacket." He pulled it out and held it up.

"That's the one," Ellie said. "It was wet on the left—sorry, his right, the jacket's right side."

Cooke put his nose near that part of the jacket and sniffed deeply. His ears went back. "There's blood on it, all right. Not much, but a good M.E. will be able to testify to it. Don't know that we can match the scent to the badger who was killed, though." He sniffed again. "If the body's not been buried, we could get a scent to compare from it, but we have to act fast."

"The carpet she was killed on is rolled up in one of the storage rooms," Ellie said. "There was some blood on it."

"Ah, that should be enough to make a match." Cooke

replaced the jacket in the back of the drawer and then stood. "And the money is in the bag, you say?"

Without waiting for an answer, he picked up the red clutch and opened it. For several seconds, he just stared. "It was last night," Ellie said, unable to see inside from her vantage point.

"It is still. I imagine she's spent some of it, but..." He shook his head and then took out a sheaf of notes. "There's a lot."

"What are you doing?" Ellie asked.

He smiled. "A trick I picked up last year. He knows how much he gave her, right? If he's just coming in to steal her money, he'd take it from the clutch and that would be that. But if he knows the amount he's looking for, he'll keep looking. Where would a girl hide extra money?"

"Under her pillow?"

"Perfect." He replaced the clutch on the dresser and then pushed the notes he'd taken from it under the pillow on the neatly made bed. "Now let's get out before too much wolf smell hangs about here."

"Open the windows," Ellie suggested. "That's why she liked this room even though she has to go through Lavinia's to get to it. It has two windows, so she could get a breeze going."

Cooke opened the windows, and then Ellie took him to the tower, where she led him carefully around the balustrade so he could see the footprints and Teddy's cane mark. "Not conclusive," he said, "but certainly important evidence. Keep this closed off. I'll have someone come around to take photographs. If they have a camera at the local constable's."

"I'm sure Mister West has one," Ellie told him.

"Good." He drew in a breath and then exhaled. "Then let's go and meet the family."

* * *

One affronted constable later, Ellie and Cooke stood in the secret passage behind her and Portia's rooms. There were two cleverly hidden eyeholes, close enough that if they pressed their heads together they could each see into the room. Ellie was nervous about being too close to him, but even though their muzzles touched, he remained perfectly courteous and kept his paws on the wall, not even near hers.

But until they heard Teddy come down the hall, there was no point in them watching the room. So they stood side by side, Cooke's ears perked toward the closed linen cupboard door, and talked only in whispers when they did.

"How long are you here for?" he asked.

"Another three weeks," she said. "My family is in Monaco."

"How is it? Apart from the murders?"

"Everyone's nice. Well, not everyone. But enough people."

"You're actually closer to Leicester here than you are at Widden's Crossing. If you want, I could take the train down some evening. If you want company."

She took a moment to think about it before answering. It felt safe; he would know she couldn't bring a guest here, and he lived a train ride away. "That would be nice," she said. "I don't know many people here."

"All right. I'll write you with my schedule."

Sergeant Cooke had been interested in her for more than a year now, and obviously he didn't know about her relationship with Abby. Because they lived apart, she'd been able to keep his courtship at arm's length. They'd met for dinner twice in that year, where she'd acted friendly but not encouraging, and he'd been patient. She got the impression there weren't many girls in Leicester for him to court, or maybe he just liked her that much.

Abby didn't mind the courtship. She knew that she and Ellie might end up with different relationships over the course of their lives and that the best they could hope for was to be in service to the same family again and to retire together. But Ellie still felt as though she'd be betraying Abby by pursuing anything else, and worse, she'd be leading on Cooke, whom she did like very much.

She could conceivably tell him the truth and then see if he still wanted to court her. But that was scary, and she much preferred lying in wait for a murderer to having that conversation.

A few minutes later, Cooke's ears perked. He hissed a soft "Shhh" as he placed his paw briefly over Ellie's, then applied his eye to the peephole. Ellie pressed forward to look through hers.

Teddy walked into Portia's room, not taking much care to be quiet. He ransacked the drawers quickly and found his jacket, then took the money from her purse on the dresser. Jacket over his arm, he counted the money, then looked around the room. A few more minutes of searching turned up the notes under the pillow, which were met with a nod of satisfaction and a confident step out of the room.

Sergeant Cooke hurried to the linen cupboard door and opened it, stepping out just in time to catch Teddy in the hall-way. "Teddy MacTavish," he said.

Before he could go on, Teddy cried, "Who the devil are you? Where did you spring from?"

"I'm Sergeant Cooke of the Royal Constabulary. You're under arrest for the murders of Georgette Hanniman and Portia Reddy."

"I—what?" Teddy sputtered. "You can't be serious. Devon confessed to—and Portia, she jumped. She's lying on the patio!"

"I'm sure the M.E. will find that she was dead when you pushed her out of the window. He's on his way here to examine the body. And Devon lied to protect you. That jacket of yours still has traces of Georgette's blood on it." After a moment, he said, "I examined it before I put it back there for you to find."

Ellie's heart pounded in the dim passageway. The silence seemed to go on forever. Then there came a choked sob, and Teddy said, "I didn't mean to. She—she called me a cripple. I just...I loved her."

What about Portia, Ellie thought. Did you not mean that one either? But Sergeant Cooke put on a gentle voice and said, "Come along, son." They passed the doorway, and their footsteps grew fainter and fainter, until even her straining ears couldn't hear them anymore.

And just like that, it was over.

CHAPTER 18
THE STAFF ROOM

The rest of the afternoon was a blur of activity, most of which Ellie missed as she was preparing supper in the kitchen (though she did have the time to say good-bye and thank you to Sergeant Cooke, and to promise, however uneasily, that she would see him in Willow's End before her time was up). She had hurried back after the arrest to finish peeling and chopping potatoes, and LeFou, when he arrived, did not criticize her work nor the amount she had done. Whether it was because she'd done a good job or because he was affected by the day's events, she didn't know, but both seemed equally unlikely. Lorna joined them soon after, and between the three of them they served supper on time to a very quiet family. "Steak au poivre," LeFou announced, "and the Duchess potatoes were prepared by Miss Stone."

For the staff, they cooked the mince in what remained of the steak au poivre sauce and served it with the potatoes. Like the family, the staff were generally quiet—even though Miss Davis was notably absent—until Ellie asked Lavinia how the rest of the afternoon had gone.

The rabbit, who had taken over many of Portia's chambermaid duties and used them as an excuse to be around the goings-on, told her that the medical examiner had come along with another officer to take Portia's body away, and that he'd said she had a head injury that didn't look like it had been caused by the fall. He confirmed the sergeant's discovery of blood on the jacket, and they also took the bloodstained carpet to compare it to.

"But none of that really matters," Ellie said, "because he confessed to the sergeant when he was arrested. He sounded really broken up over it."

"About Portia?" Lavinia asked.

"Well—no." Ellie looked around at the other staff. LeFou sat eating the meal without any indication that he was listening to the conversation. "About Georgette."

"Poor Portia," one of the others said.

"If Portia's gone," William said loudly, "when are we going to get another one?"

"Hush." Lorna put a paw on his arm. "In a week or so, perhaps."

Lavinia lifted her glass. "To Portia," she said, and the staff all raised a glass to her. The rest of the supper was spent telling stories about Portia to remember her. Everyone had multiple stories, and even William said that she'd been kind to him. The talk turned to when or where there would be a memorial service for her. Nobody quite knew who was to arrange that.

"She had family in London," Ellie said, and at that point Miss Davis swept into the room and put a stop to the conversation.

"There have been a number of unfortunate events in this house over the last few days," she said. "I want to commend all of you for getting your work done through these difficulties. Without Portia and Devon, we will have some challenges until replacements can be found. Lavinia will take over as the head parlourmaid—"

"What?" Lavinia had clearly not been consulted about this change.

"You've been a parlourmaid for six years," Miss Davis said. "You've been at Fortescue longer than any of the others. I'm certain you can manage."

Lavinia bit her bottom lip and looked pouty but stayed silent. The other two maids looked equally uncertain, but none of them challenged Miss Davis. She turned to Ellie. "I'm also bringing a message that Mister West would like to see you in his study when you've finished clearing supper. He said," and here she glanced at LeFou, "to make sure you had discharged all your kitchen duties before coming."

The fox gave a short sniff and a tail-flick and kept eating. Ellie nodded. "Yes'm."

The staff finished their meal mostly in silence, and then Ellie and Lorna gathered the dishes, with William helping. LeFou cast a critical eye over the kitchen as they piled the dishes near the sink. "Wash the pans," he said, "and then Miss Stone, you are released. Lorna and William can finish the dishes and dry and replace everything."

"He likes you," Lorna commented when he'd gone.

"I don't think he likes anyone." Ellie took the first pan. "Except perhaps Mister West."

"He doesn't like Mister West," Lorna told her, passing along the steel wool.

"What? But they talk so often."

"He understands him." This was the most Lorna had ever spoken to Ellie. "He says that Mister West also seeks out recipes, but his ingredients are people."

"What does that mean, I wonder."

"I think it means that, you know, LeFou takes ingredients and decides what dish can be made of them, and Mister West looks at people and figures out how they go together. Like when he unearths cities, it's as if he was tasting a dish and then figuring out what went into it."

"Oh." Ellie thought about that. "That's clever. But LeFou doesn't like him?"

"He says Mister West does not have a discerning palate and he..." Here she lowered her voice. "He spends too much time in the business of others. But he likes Callie. He says she has good taste and isn't afraid to say it. And I think he likes you. You're very clever and you can cook."

Ellie scrubbed at the pot and thought of what to say to that. "If you're not happy here, Lorna, you could find another position. I might be leaving mine next year. I could put in a word for you."

"Not happy here?" The wildcat looked surprised.

"I thought—but he treats you so poorly in the kitchen."

Lorna nodded. "I'm not very good in the kitchen. But I'm learning, and who better could I learn from?"

She had put a slight stress on "kitchen," but Ellie didn't ask for clarification and Lorna gave none.

When the pans had been duly scrubbed, Ellie dried her paws, took off her apron, and walked down the hall to Mister West's study. She walked quickly, with a nervous excitement that she couldn't quite explain. The case was solved, the murderer in custody. What was left to be nervous about? But when she was working to solve a case, her mind was occupied; now she had nothing to think about except what Mister West would say to her.

She passed the library and remembered her first day here, when she'd surprised Bonnie reading something in the library, a book Bonnie had wanted to hide from her. Her mind, anxious for something else to seize on, thought about the things Bonnie had said to her then, and put them together with some other things Ellie had heard over the last week. Three more steps, and the situation clicked into focus in the way those things did when you hadn't been thinking about them for a while. "Oh," she said to herself. "So that's what she was reading."

Having worked out a problem she hadn't even realized was a problem calmed her down. Her tail stopped flicking around, and when she arrived at Mister West's study, she knocked confidently.

"Come," he called, and she walked into the now-familiar room, closing the door behind her. He gestured to a chair, and she took a seat.

"I must say," he said, "you've exceeded my expectations. As a detective's assistant, that is. Your cooking is good, but not better than it was represented to me." His eyes twinkled at her.

"Thank you, sir," she said. "I'm very sorry for your family. And Georgette's and Portia's."

"Of course," he replied, his smile returning to a more somber expression. "Thank you. It's been a trying day—a trying week, really—but your help has proved invaluable. I admit I never would have thought it of Teddy. Not the Georgette thing —he has a temper—but killing Portia."

"I don't know if he said anything," Ellie ventured, "but I was thinking about that while making dinner. He was paying her off, and that should've been the end of it. But she hadn't cleaned the jacket, and he would've known that when she didn't set it back in his room. And what's more, she was talking about the money she'd come into. Portia was very talkative and not a very good liar, which is a bad combination for a blackmailer."

Mister West nodded. "They may not charge him with her death, that's what your sergeant told me. It will be difficult to prove. With Georgette, they have the blood and the confession, and so the other matter is rather beside the point."

Ellie, emboldened by her detective work, said, "Excuse me,

sir, but I don't think it is beside the point. A person was murdered. And that one was planned ahead of time, not accidental like Georgette's. She'll have a head injury from his cane, and he took the money from her purse and under the pillow, which means he knew exactly how much he'd given her, and we saw the mark of his cane on the roof."

He started to say something with a frown, then considered her words and gave a nod. "The issue, I was told, was whether someone in Portia's family wants charges brought. After all, she was blackmailing her employer. Her family might not want that to come out in court."

"Oh. I hadn't thought of that."

He nodded. "Sergeant Cooke promised to look up her family in London and get word to them. It would be possible for us to press the charges, as her employer, but I declined to do that. I am also Teddy's great-uncle, which puts me in a difficult position."

"I'll testify, if it comes to that," Ellie said boldly.

"I'm certain you will." He smiled, but there was sadness in it. "I do wonder whether I've done enough to keep my family together here."

"I think," Ellie said, "that if your sister forgives you when Bonnie joins your dig, you needn't worry about how she reacts to her grandson's trial."

He straightened with a jerk and stared at her. "How can you possibly know that?" he asked in a low voice.

"I didn't," she said with some satisfaction. "Not until just now. But it was the most likely case."

Mister West leaned forward. "Based on what?"

Ellie rested her paws on her knees, her tail twitching again. She forced back the nervousness under his scrutiny. "I surprised her in the library reading a book she didn't want me to see. I suppose it was one of yours, but I didn't think of that then. And then she said something that stuck with me, that if there were a problem and she or you weren't around, I should see Miss Davis."

"That's right," he said. "Why is that odd?"

"It's only the boys who go off to London," she said. "Bonnie's here for every meal. So are you. The only place you're going is to a dig in two weeks, I think?" He nodded. "By itself it didn't mean anything, but she linked herself and you when she said it, and so in my head I was thinking you'd be going somewhere together."

"But that could be anywhere. Or she could be in London after I leave for the dig."

Ellie nodded. "Your sister came to the kitchen one day to warn me not to pay too much attention to your 'flights of fancy,' I think she called them. And she didn't think much of your archaeology."

Mister West laced his fingers together in front of himself and sighed. "She resents my success and her lack of it."

"So it made sense that Bonnie would hide that she was interested in your digs. But Wilkins was the one who put it all together for me."

"Wilkins?" His eyes widened. "Did he see—how did he do that?"

"She's been digging in the garden, hasn't she?" Ellie smiled when Mister West nodded. "Wilkins thinks it's cubs from the village, but it's in an out of the way spot that he wouldn't normally have found, and he never catches them. As if they know when he'll be in the garden."

"Ah."

"That's who was in the garden when we were on the roof, wasn't it?" she asked. "I couldn't quite tell, but you said it was nothing, and I was more worried about Portia then."

"Yes," he said. "Bonnie's been practicing digging up pottery carefully in the backyard. It's silly, but she wanted to do it."

"I couldn't work out who in the household would be digging there, or what they might be burying, but when your sister was so disdainful of your accomplishments...I figured it was one of her children. Finley's in London all the time and Todd and Teddy's parents aren't here."

He shook his head with a rueful smile. "You continue to impress me, Miss Stone. I must ask your discretion in this matter. Callie thinks Bonnie is going to vacation with a friend from school."

"Of course," Ellie said. "It's not my place to say anything."

"Speaking of that," he said, "I hope you will use discretion about tonight's dinner."

He assumed she'd been listening at the servery, but tonight she had not. When she thought back, though, she remembered Todd's raised voice coming through even to the kitchen. "Of course, sir," she said, playing along. "About Todd, you mean?"

"Yes." He drummed fingers on his desk. "I think I have talked him into going back to the bank on Monday. It turns out that he had been getting some tranquilizers to help with a nervous disposition, but he, er, cannot get them any longer."

"Georgette had been bringing them," Ellie guessed.

"Yes."

"She made herself useful around here." Ellie shook her head. "I never guessed how many people's lives she touched."

"Er, yes. I suppose that's true. In any case, his nervousness got the better of him tonight, what with the murders and all, and his raving about being as bad as his brother—well, he's just been in Teddy's shadow all his life. Stayed behind while Teddy went to war, saw his brother come back a wounded hero, and now his hero is a murderer and his tranquilizers are gone. Poor fellow." His gaze fell to his desk.

"Will he be all right?"

Mister West looked up. "Oh, yes, I suppose so. I'll have a

prescription written in London, so he can pick it up after his job and nobody local need know about it. He'll be fine."

Ellie had meant about his brother being a murderer, but she kept that quiet. "I'm glad to hear it."

"Well, have you solved any other mysteries here at Fortescue Hall?" he asked with that twinkle returning to his eye.

"No," she said. "I still don't know what Finley does when he comes back by the earlier train. I suppose it *was* him and not Todd that I saw in the hall that day, because Todd doesn't lie about what train he takes. I still don't know why he—Finley, I mean—would come back here and not tell anyone."

"Ah." He looked very satisfied with himself. "I suspect it was raining in London that day."

"What?"

He sat back and folded his paws over his stomach. "You will have to tell me if you make any progress."

"I will, but I hardly ever see Finley."

Mister West nodded. "It is a more difficult case, but that is to be expected." He leaned forward again. "I called you here to tell you about the resolution of the case, and to thank you for the fine detective work you did. If you ever feel you have outgrown the kitchen, I think the police force could find a place for you."

"Oh, I could never." Her ears warmed and her tail flicked. "You solved the case as much as I did, sir."

He wagged a finger at her. "That sort of humility befits an assistant cook, but not a detective's sergeant. Accept the credit for what you've done."

"All right." Her ears warmed further. "Thank you, sir."

"I don't leave for another two weeks. I expect we will have more conversations. But thank you, Miss Stone."

"You're welcome, sir." She stood to leave.

"Oh, Miss Stone?"

She turned. "Sir?"

"The potatoes were excellent. I don't know anyone else who could solve a murder and prepare Duchess potatoes in the same day. Well done."

"Thank you, sir." She couldn't keep the smile from her muzzle as she hurried out of the room.

CHAPTER 19
THE SUN ROOM

L ife at Fortescue Hall settled down somewhat after that. Without Teddy or Devon, things were quieter in general, but even Callie's sharp tongue seemed subdued, and James did not attempt to pull Ellie into a game of cards. He still told her long stories, but they seemed more wistful, many of them around when Teddy and Todd were just cubs.

Todd went to the bank the next week, every day, and at the end of the week Ellie overheard Finley telling the family at dinner that Todd was doing very well. Bonnie kept to herself but favored Ellie with a smile whenever their paths crossed.

Lavinia tried her best to take over Portia's responsibilities, but every evening in the midst of complaining to Ellie about all the new tasks she had, she remembered one she'd forgotten and had to run out to take care of it. Ellie often helped when she could

LeFou, of all the people in the house, treated Ellie exactly the same as he ever had, with withering scorn when she made a mistake (which happened rarely) and with silent approval when she did well. He treated Lorna the same way, but one evening as he was preparing a roast lamb shank, Ellie caught Lorna watching him, and the adoring look in the wildcat's eyes explained much. Sometimes, she told herself, people will endure anything to be near someone they love or respect, or both, and that was none of Ellie's business. But she made life easier for Lorna when she could, and the wildcat did seem to respond better to Ellie's soft touch than to LeFou's sharp one, at least as far as learning kitchen tasks went.

After the second week, Miss Davis called Ellie into the sun room after Saturday luncheon. The tall rabbit had also been very busy over the past week, and Ellie suspected she was covering some of Lavinia's work.

There were three chairs and a divan in the sun room, but Miss Davis remained standing and so Ellie did also. The sun was just coming in, illuminating the soft green carpet and the geraniums in a pretty crystal vase on the end table. Out in the garden, Wilkins was tending to one of the flowerbeds, moving slowly through them on his knees, pulling weeds and putting them into a bag at his side.

"I called you here," Miss Davis said, "to give you a mid-way update on your progress."

"Yes'm." Ellie focused her attention on the rabbit.

Miss Davis took a small notebook out of her pocket and flipped it open to a page. "Your primary duties have been in the kitchen, and you have done well there. I have noticed an improvement after two weeks, and LeFou..." Her nose wrinkled as she said the name. "Says the same. Very satisfactory."

"Thank you, ma'am," Ellie said.

"And then there is the matter of..." Miss Davis hesitated. "Last week's unpleasantness. While you certainly exceeded your authority on a number of occasions and demonstrated a familiarity with the family that is not at all appropriate...particularly Mister West, though I am aware that he encouraged this, still, it cannot be denied that you pursued justice for one of your own when perhaps the local authorities would not have gone to such lengths. Bringing in an outside police sergeant was not the course I would have taken, but in the event, it did serve to limit the gossip in the town and ultimately benefited the family." She looked up at Ellie. "Therefore, we will mark you 'satisfactory' in that matter as well."

"Thank you, ma'am."

"Lastly, there is the personal matter I approached you about." She lowered her voice. "Here again I must report mixed results. Due to circumstances, Lavinia has been thrust into more responsibility than perhaps she is ready for. She has attempted to meet that responsibility, but...I cannot say that she is..." She sighed and closed the notebook, pushing it back into her pocket. "She isn't doing a good job. I cannot talk around it. However, I cannot lay this at your feet. I have seen you helping her, and I know you are doing all you can do to help."

Ellie nodded. "She is overwhelmed."

"Therefore, if things continue as they have been, I will be happy to write you a positive recommendation," Miss Davis said. "Have you any questions or anything to say?"

"Just one thing, if I may." Ellie's heart beat faster at the idea of a good recommendation and what it might mean, but she could celebrate that later. She reached into her own pocket and took out a piece of paper. She unfolded it carefully and held it out.

"What is this?" Miss Davis took it, and her breath caught. "Is this—?"

"It's Portia," Ellie confirmed. "Your daughter drew that."

Miss Davis continued to look at it without speaking. Ellie went on. "If Lavinia hadn't been drawing, we might not have caught Teddy. Accidentally, of course I understand that, but she was in our room and so he couldn't get into Portia's to get his jacket before we were ready. I know Lavinia wants to please you—"

"Hah." Miss Davis said.

"—but she has a gift for art. And she does not seem to have a gift for housework, not as you do."

"Art is not a steady career." Miss Davis gave the picture back to Ellie. "People will always need their rooms cleaned and clothes washed, but art? I don't want her to turn out like—"

She stopped abruptly. Ellie waited a moment and then asked, gently, "Like her father?"

"Her father died before she was born," Miss Davis said brusquely. "He was a 'bohemian,' I believe the term is, with no interest in providing for a family. I had to provide for her and raise her myself."

"I understand," Ellie said. "Of course you're her mother and you know what's best. I'm simply showing you her talent. It would be a shame to waste it."

"She may continue to draw in the evenings," Miss Davis said. "Thank you, Miss Stone. You are dismissed."

Ellie gave a quick nod, turned, and walked to the door. But when she looked back from there, Miss Davis was still staring out at the garden, lost in thought. *I did what I could,* Ellie thought. *Rome wasn't built in a day.*

* * *

A few days later, Ellie was summoned to Mister West's study between breakfast and lunch. She found him sitting behind his desk in a crisp yellow shirt with a red bowtie and suspenders, wire-frame glasses perched on his muzzle. Diffuse light from the cloudy day outside lit the room, highlighting the grey hairs around the edges of his ears. "Ah," he said cheerfully, "come in, Miss Stone. Please, have a seat."

Ellie sat in one of the chairs before the great oak desk. "Thank you, sir," she said. "What may I do for you?"

"Bonnie and I will be leaving tomorrow," the old badger said, "and I wanted to let you know how much I've appreciated your presence here the last few weeks. I'm told Miss Davis will be writing you an excellent recommendation."

"Thank you, sir." Ellie's ears warmed. "I'm glad to have been useful."

"And I have a question for you. You strike me as someone who keeps her eyes and ears open. How do you feel the household has responded to Teddy's arrest?"

Ellie took a moment to compose herself. "I couldn't say, sir. I would imagine you would know better than I would."

"I wish I did." He drummed his thick claws on the desk. "Todd wrote to his parents, and so did Callie. They've received responses, but I don't know what they said or if they're coming back soon. Todd spends more time in London but won't say what he's doing there."

"I'm sure I haven't heard anything, sir," Ellie said.

"Ah." He looked disappointed. "I thought you might have. Tell me, Miss Stone, is there anyone among the staff who might have their ear to the ground, as it were?"

What an odd request. But Ellie thought she was beginning to understand Mister West a little more. "I couldn't say, sir. The kitchen staff mostly keep to the kitchen. I would say Miss Davis probably knows the household best."

He nodded. "Yes, Miss Davis. Ah, well."

"Miss Davis does not approve of gossip," Ellie said.

The old badger peered at her over his spectacles. He smiled. "No, she does not."

"And," Ellie guessed, "she is not well disposed to Mr. LeFou, even if she did."

He didn't respond to that, but his smile and silence told her she'd been right, that LeFou had gathered household gossip and brought it to him. Portia had likely been LeFou's source, because the fox had not visited Mister West's study more than twice in the two weeks since her death, and now Mister West was asking Ellie who the household gossip was. Portia herself had not gossiped to Mister West—Miss Davis would have had a fit—but she'd said LeFou was always kind to her, and Ellie recalled LeFou telling Mister West something Portia had seen but hadn't understood.

"Well, Miss Stone, it has been a great pleasure, as I said," Mister West said finally. "I hope the remainder of your stay at Fortescue is very pleasant indeed." And he lowered his head to his desk, an obvious dismissal.

"If I may, sir, on the subject of Lavinia?"

He lifted his head. "Yes?"

"Did you know she intends to go to art school?"

"I know she applied. I have not heard whether she has been accepted."

"She was. The day Georgette was killed." Ellie took a breath. "She may have some trouble arranging the funds to attend—"

Mister West stopped her with a raised paw. "I cannot pay for her schooling. What would people say? And Miss Davis would be deeply hurt. She might even give her notice."

"I understand, sir." Ellie rubbed her paws together. "But you might put in a good word with Miss Davis. I showed her some of Lavinia's art. She is so talented, Lavinia, I mean, and if Miss Davis thought you approved, then she might..."

He studied her thoughtfully. "She might indeed. Well, we are already inquiring for another lead parlourmaid. I can have Mildred—Miss Davis—also inquire about another maid position."

"Thank you, sir. It would mean the world to Lavinia." Ellie stood, curtseyed, and walked to the door.

"Miss Stone!" the old badger called as she laid a paw on the doorknob.

She turned. "Yes, sir?"

"I have not been able to discover to whom you have been writing letters, and it struck me just now that this may be my last chance."

Ellie stood for a moment, gazing back at his eager expression, and said, "That is a personal matter, sir." With that, she left the study.

CHAPTER 20
THE SOMERLEYTON
PINT (REVISITED)

My dearest Abby,

Of course you are right. I knew you would say the right thing. I love you so much. I've invited Sergeant Cooke down, and I'll take your advice. I'll write to you again after our dinner to tell you everything about it.

Mister West and Bonnie left today, supposedly for different destinations even though they left by the same train. James and Callie told Bonnie to call them when she arrived in Santorini, and Bonnie, who knew I kept their secret, confided in me that her school friend has been instructed to answer the phone as if she is there but busy anytime her parents call. She will then call Bonnie at the dig and Bonnie will call them back. It's rather a lot of work to avoid angering one's parents, but I can well understand it.

We will be getting a new head parlourmaid on Monday. Miss Davis rang up the service and today went to Coventry to interview the candidates herself. We haven't heard, but she is so efficient that I am certain she will find someone.

Lavinia has been mostly a disaster in that job, but she is not upset about it at all. If anything, she's cross that it's taken two weeks for her mother to proclaim her a disaster. Miss Davis told me last Saturday that she was giving up despite my help, but that she appreciated it. And she's going to write me a good recommendation! This time next year, Abby dear, I might be working in your house's kitchen!

Oh, you'll never believe this. At dinner last night, we served roast pheasant with cheese and onion pasties. I made the puff pastry for the pasties myself and I even helped with the pheasant, and when we served it, LeFou just said, "I've prepared a roast pheasant, plus cheese and onion pasties and buttered beans and peas." Every meal he's told them which part of the meal I made, but not this time. We've been getting along better this last week, so I asked him about it when we were back in the kitchen, and he said that my pasties were good enough that he would put his name to them. He sounded like I should be honored.

In a strange way, I suppose I am. I've learned so much here, and my cooking is definitely better than it was. But I won't miss working in that kitchen. The fox is a genius but he's also impossible. He won't actually give me any of the recipes we've made, so I've had to go back and write them down as I remember them. I will definitely make these cheese and onion pasties for you the next time we get to see each other.

And I hope that's soon, old soul. I miss you greatly.

All my love,

Ellie

* * *

The Somerleyton Pint was busier on this Friday night than it had been the night she'd been here with Portia, but Ellie liked that. Three weeks in Willow's End had left her feeling attached to the small town, and a busy pub reflected well on it for Sergeant Cooke. Besides that, the elevated murmur of more people made their conversation feel more private.

She'd already introduced him to Betsy at the newspaper

stand as "the officer who helped catch Georgette's murderer," and Betsy had given her fellow wolf a big, tearful hug. He'd smiled and patted her and said all the right things, and though he stayed professional, the first thing he'd said when they sat down was, "It's not often we get to meet someone after an arrest like that. Reminds one of the difference one can make, doesn't it?"

Ellie nodded as Cross came over to the table. "Well," the black rat said, "Miss Stone has a new companion."

"This is my friend Sergeant Cooke of the Leicester Police," Ellie said.

At the word "police," a few heads turned. Cross's ears flicked, but he remained polite as Cooke extended a paw to him. "Off duty," he said. "Purely a social call."

"Well, enjoy your time in Willow's End," Cross said. "If you like ale, Black Sheep is a fine local one. Would be my pleasure to offer you one on the house."

"Thank you, sir. I'm told you don't offer much food, but your steak and kidney pie is worth trying."

Cross shot a smile at Ellie. "Ah, sir, we can get food from Miss June's next door if our patrons want it. The steak and kidney is the best, as Miss Stone well knows."

"I'll have some of that, then."

"And I as well," Ellie said.

"And your usual drink?" the rat asked, and Ellie nodded. "And sir, there's a smoke room in the back for chaps that like a good pipe."

The wolf tapped his long muzzle. "I appreciate the offer, but I don't smoke."

"Of course. Just thought I'd let you know."

When he'd left, Cooke said, "You've really settled in here, haven't you?"

"You helped a bit," Ellie told him. "After we arrested Teddy, well—it wasn't that people liked Georgette, but they did like

Portia. Especially here. And they like Mister West, but not his family as much. Except one of them. So it went over well that we arrested one of the children for the murder of someone they genuinely liked."

The wolf looked around the inn. "Seems a good bunch here. Glad you've got on well with them, but sorry it was about a murder, of course."

Then Ellie asked about his work, and he asked about hers. She told him about the dubious honor conferred on her by LeFou, and in the meantime their drinks came, and presently the steak and kidney pie.

Ellie found it very pleasant to be sitting with the Sergeant. He talked about police work easily enough, but also about his family and friends, and he listened to her talking about her family as well. They had read some of the same police novels and were in the middle of discussing one of them when Ellie caught movement at the corner of the bar. "Oh," she said in a low voice. "There's Finley MacTavish. He's Teddy's uncle."

Cooke turned to look. "I don't remember you mentioning him in the case."

Ellie shifted a little so that Cooke would hide her from Finley's gaze—she hoped. "He wasn't at home when Portia was killed. He comes here instead of going home after work, and we can't figure out why. Oh," she said. "Maybe he comes here to smoke? But I don't remember him smelling like smoke when he came by the table."

"Are there rooms upstairs?"

Ellie thought back. "There must be. There's a second story."

"He's meeting someone the family wouldn't approve of, then. That's what it's got to be."

"Oh." Her ears warmed. "I should've thought that—I did think that when I thought he was meeting Portia. But he wasn't, and then I didn't...oh!"

"What is it? You know who he's meeting?"

Ellie shook her head. "No, but Mister West said...it was raining in London. Of course that's what happened. He got mud on his clothes and came back to Fortescue to change, the day Georgette was killed. But he snuck out again, so he didn't want anyone to have seen him. Tch." She frowned. "I should have figured that out."

Cooke turned back to the table. "Keep your eyes there and let me know who comes out next."

The trick was not to stare at that corner, because Cross seemed to have a bartender's sixth sense that let him know when someone was looking at the bar. Still, she managed to keep it in her vision as she kept talking to Cooke. Finley remained there, drinking his ale, and when he'd finished, he paid Cross and left.

Not two minutes after he'd gone, a short hedgehog walked out from the same corner of the bar. He wore a dapper green suit and a blue ascot, and a small bowler hat that he kept adjusting. Cross nodded to him as he walked past the bar, and the hedgehog inclined his head.

"There's someone," Ellie said. "Oh. Do you think he was meeting that hedgehog?"

She said it without thinking through the implications of the statement, but by the time Cooke turned to look, her stomach was already twisting itself in knots in anticipatory dread. But he didn't react with disgust or with shock, only the satisfied nod of a detective solving a mystery. "That would fit," he said. "I doubt the family would sanction that kind of thing. It goes on rather often, though, you know. There's a chap in the constabulary who's an 'artistic type,' you know? We all know about him, but it would be a frightful scandal if it came out in public. Poor fellow."

Relief washed over her. She thought about what Abby had written, and it felt more possible than it ever had in the past. So she composed herself and said, "Someone in my old family was like that too. He went to school in America and came back, but eventually said he felt more comfortable back there."

"That makes sense. Not that it's easier there, but..." The wolf waved. "Harder to have secrets in small towns like this."

Ellie nodded. "Um," she said in a low voice. "I know...there are ladies like that too."

Sergeant Cooke nodded, having taken another bite of the steak and kidney pie. When he'd swallowed, he said, "I've heard that, but I never knew any. I'm not privy to many ladies' secrets, you know." And he smiled broadly at her.

She leaned forward. "Can I tell you one of mine?"

He nodded and extended his paw across the table. "I would love that."

His paw was tempting, but...what if she grasped it and then he pulled away when he heard? If you trust him, then trust him, Abby had said, and Ellie smiled, recalling those words. She let her fingers touch his, and he curled his paw around hers. "I'm...one of those ladies," she said.

It was like hearing someone else say the words, only then she had to experience the aftermath. His smile froze, then hitched, and he inclined his head. "No. Really?"

But his paw didn't let go. Ellie nodded. "Really. I have a friend..." She lowered her eyes, ears warming.

"Oh," he said. Still his paw held hers.

"I didn't mean to lead you on," she said quickly. "I like you, I really do. But I couldn't honestly...and it's just difficult...I didn't want to deceive you."

"You haven't," he said quickly. "You know, in our detective training they warn us not to make assumptions. Anything I thought about you that you didn't tell me is an assumption, and that's on me."

"But still," Ellie said.

"Hush." Now he squeezed her paw. "Miss Stone, you're remarkable, and this does explain why no other fellow has managed to scoop you up yet. Let me ask you, though, why not simply turn me down?"

"Because I do like you." She sighed. "I was afraid if I turned you down, I wouldn't get to see you anymore. And I enjoy your company. But I can't promise myself to you entirely."

"Heh." He tapped a finger against the paw he held. "I haven't asked you to, have I?"

"No," she said. "But that's often what lies down the end of this road."

"Now who's making assumptions?" he teased.

Her laugh came out almost as a hiccup. "Really? You weren't courting me with an eye to marriage?"

"I admit the possibility had crossed my mind, but I think you're a fascinating person and I just wanted to spend time getting to know you. And I've done that. It is more rewarding than I'd hoped."

This warmed her ears again. Her stomach still fluttered, but it wasn't a bad feeling. "Really?"

"Indeed."

"You're a decent liar, you know," she told him.

He laughed. "About what? Getting to know you?"

"About the possibility of marriage only 'crossing your mind.'"

"All right," he said. "Perhaps I envisioned us as a husband-and-wife detective team. It was an attractive fantasy, you must admit."

"I can see that."

He gave her paw another squeeze and then released it, settling back. "So have you told your...friend...about me?"

She nodded. "She's the one who insisted I tell you. She's very sweet, and also very clever when it comes to...well, I don't know how to say it. Not like detective-clever, but she knows people."

"And she knows me?"

"Oh, yes, well...you met her at the St. Clair's. Where we first met. She was in service there with me."

The wolf blinked and then tapped the table thoughtfully. "I have a good memory, but I'm afraid I can't reach back and remember everyone who was there. The family were foxes, I know that, and there was another weasel, and a deer, and a dhole? No, the dhole was a chap, wasn't he? Never mind," he said as she opened her mouth. "It's not important. But maybe someday I'll meet her and thank her."

"Thank her?"

He nodded. "Because I get to see the real you. More of you, anyway."

"Oh." Ellie smiled. "I'm glad you like the real me."

"Of course. And..." He reached across the table again, and this time she took his paw without hesitation. "I know it must have been hard to tell me. Thank you, Miss Stone."

"Thank you for...for understanding."

The wolf squeezed her paw again and then released it to return to his steak and kidney pie. "I wish I had something that significant to tell you about myself. Alas, my biggest secret is that my previous engagement ended because of me, not because of her."

"You were engaged?" Ellie's stomach settled with the changing of the subject.

He nodded. "To the daughter of friends of my parents. But she had no curiosity, and I could not see making her part of my life. I agreed to put out the story that she had rejected me, because a rejected fellow is not such an oddity, but a rejected lady will always have future suitors wonder what was wrong with her. Such is our world. As it happened, she was engaged again within the year. She has two lovely cubs now."

"That's nice," Ellie said.

"And that's my sordid past, all of it."

"I think it was a noble thing to do. And I admire your search for brains in a lady. Not many fellows are too interested in that."

"The pleasures of the flesh too soon pass away," he declaimed, "and what remains is what sustains." At her raised eyebrows, he splayed his ears and grinned abashedly. "It's not Shakespeare or anything. It was an advice column in a newspaper. But it has stayed with me."

"It's good advice," Ellie said.

"I thought so. And I think, you know, it can also apply to friendships where the pleasures of the flesh are never, ah, part of it. In a way, they've passed away already."

"Cheers, then." Ellie raised her glass. "To friendship."

"And to more murders solved in the future." Cooke raised his glass and clinked hers.

"Even if we're not husband and wife," Ellie said. "I still think we make a good team."

ABOUT THE AUTHOR

Kyell Gold has won thirteen Ursa Major awards and a Cóyotl Award for his stories and novels, and his acclaimed novel "Out of Position" co-won the Rainbow Award for Best Gay Novel of 2009. He helped create RAWR, the first residential furry writing workshop, and has instructed at each of its sessions through 2022.

He lives in California, loves to travel and dine out with his partners (when possible), and can be seen at furry conventions around the world. More information about him and his books is available at http://www.kyellgold.com.

patreon.com/kyellgold

bsky.app/profile/kyellgold.com

furries.club/@kyellgold

substack.com/@kyellgold

ABOUT THE ARTIST

Irene is an illustrator dedicated to crafting narrative-driven scenes defined by evocative colors. Her portfolio emphasizes a deep passion for depicting creatures and the natural world.
https://www.irenehuang.com

ALSO BY KYELL GOLD

If you would like to get monthly updates on upcoming publications, excerpts of works in progress, and writing tips, sign up for his mailing list (your e-mail address will not be sold or used for anything else).

Love Match

Love Match (vol. 1, 2008-2010) — Rocky arrives in the States from Africa and navigates the treacherous worlds of professional tennis and high school.

Love Match (vol. 2, 2010-2012) — Rocky begins his professional career, at the cost of his family and romantic relationships.

Love Match (vol. 3, 2013-2015) — As his career trends upward, Rocky's romantic life becomes less stable.

Out of Position (Dev and Lee)

Out of Position – Dev the football player and Lee the gay activist discover how to navigate their relationship. *(mature readers)*

Isolation Play – The continuing story of Dev and Lee, as they contend with family and friends in their search for acceptance. *(mature readers)*

Divisions – As Dev's team fights to make the playoffs, Lee fights to keep his sense of self. *(mature readers)*

Uncovered – The playoffs are here, and Dev needs his focus more than ever. So when Lee becomes too distracting, something has to give. *(mature readers)*

Over Time – Dev and Lee try to plan their future while dealing with crises all around them. *(mature readers)*

Ty Game — Dev's teammate Ty navigates an arranged marriage while also falling in love. *(mature readers)*

Tales of the Firebirds — A collection of stories exploring the lives of some of the other characters from the Out of Position series. *(mature readers)*

Titles – In the two weeks leading up to Dev's third try at a championship, Dev and Lee face new challenges and changes in their lives. *(mature readers)*

Dangerous Spirits

Green Fairy – A gay high school senior struggling through his final year finds a strange old book that changes his dreams and his life.

Red Devil – A gay fox who fled his abusive family in Siberia seeks help from a ghost who demands he give up his gay lifestyle.

Black Angel – A young otter struggles to understand her sexuality as her friends prepare for post-high school life and dreams of women in other times plague her.

Argaea

Volle – The story of how Volle came to Tephos, a spy masquerading as a noble, and the first adventure he had there. *(mature readers)*

The Prisoner's Release and Other Stories – The story of how Volle escaped from prison, and the story of what happened after, plus two other stories following characters from "Volle." *(mature readers)*

Pendant of Fortune – Volle returns to Tephos to defend his honor, but soon finds himself fighting for much more. *(mature readers)*

Shadow of the Father – Volle's son, Yilon, must travel to the far-off land he is meant to rule, but he will have to fight treachery to take the lordship. *(mature readers)*

Weasel Presents – Five short stories from the land of Argaea, including "Helfer's Busy Day" and "Yilon's Journal." *(mature readers)*

Return From Divalia — Years after a night of adventure ruined his life, a young wolf gets a chance at redemption. *(mature readers, coming 2022)*

Forester Universe

Waterways – The full story of Kory's journey to understand himself and what it means to be gay. *(mature readers)*

Bridges – Hayward seems content to set up pairs of his friends. But what does he really need for himself? *(mature readers)*

Science Friction – Vaxy never took sex seriously, until he found out the professor he was sleeping with was married... *(mature readers)*

Winter Games – Sierra Snowpaw was an unsure high school student when someone he thought was a friend changed his life. Now he's fifteen years older and still looking for answers. *(mature readers)*

The Mysterious Affair of Giles – A servant in a British manor house tries to solve a murder.

Dude, Where's My Fox? – Lonnie chases down a fox he hooked up with at a party as a way to get over his breakup. *(mature readers)*

Dude, Where's My Pack? — Lonnie tries to navigate relationships old and new. *(mature readers)*

Losing My Religion – On tour with his R.E.M. cover band, Jackson mentors the new guy in the band as his own life falls apart. *(mature readers)*

The Time He Desires — A Muslim immigrant struggles with the betrayal of his son and the dissolution of his marriage, as well as his own long-past trauma.

Camouflage — When Danilo is sent 500 years into the past, he must choose between safety in an unfamiliar world and his own sense of what is right. *(mature readers)*

Other Books

The Silver Circle – Valerie thought the old hunter was crazy when he warned her about werewolves—until she met one.

In the Doghouse of Justice – Seven stories of superheroes and their not-so-super relationships. *(mature readers)*

Twelve Sides — Twelve short stories about side characters from the above books. *(mature readers)*

Do You Need Help? — Writing advice for furry (and non-furry) writers.

Writing as Tim Susman:

Breaking The Ice: Stories from New Tibet (editor) - On a hostile ice planet, survival is guaranteed to nobody.

Shadows in Snow (editor) - More stories from the unforgiving ice world of New Tibet.

Common and Precious - A kidnapped heiress comes to sympathize with her desperate captors, while her father discovers the limits of his power in trying to rescue her.

THE CALATIANS

Book 1: The Tower and the Fox - Kip and his friends encounter prejudice and mysteries in their first few months at Prince George's College of Sorcery.

Book 2: The Demon and the Fox - The forces of revolution grow in Massachusetts as Kip and his friends rush to solve the mystery of the attack on the College of Sorcery.

Book 3: The War and the Fox - Kip and his friends are drafted into the fight for independence from Britain, but there is more at stake.

Book 4: The Revolution and the Fox - Two years after the war, Kip and his friends face their greatest threat yet.

Other books

Unfinished Business — A detective uncovers a plot against him and must turn to his werewolf ex-boyfriend for help.

The Price of Thorns - A down-on-his-luck thief meets the actual evil queen from many fairy tales when she offers him the job of a lifetime. (Coming 2023)